Deadly Discrimination

a Fr. Jake Mystery

Albert Noyer

Books by Albert Noyer

The Saint's Day Deaths (2000)
The Secundus Papyrus (2003)
The Cybelene Conspiracy (2005)
The Ghosts of Glorieta: A Fr. Jake Mystery (2011)
One for the Money, Two for the Sluice: A Fr. Jake Mystery (2013)
Death at Pergamum (2013) Kindle
Unholy Sepulcher (2014) Kindle
Alberix the Celt, Book 1: Weep the Long Sorrow (2014)
Alberix the Celt, Book 2: Hear Again the Lark (2015)
The Kashat Deception (2015) Kindle

Deadly Discrimination

a Fr. Jake Mystery

Albert Noyer

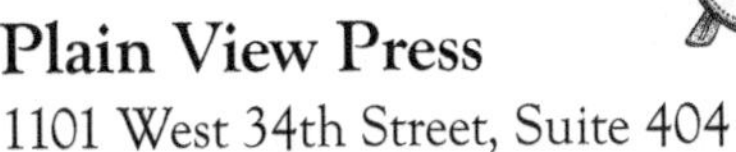

Plain View Press
1101 West 34th Street, Suite 404

http://plainviewpress.net
Austin, TX 78705

ISBN: 978-1-63210-093-1
Library of Congress Control Number: 2021941916

Cover design by Albert Noyer

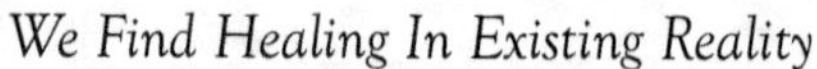

We Find Healing In Existing Reality

Plain View Press is a 36-year-old issue-based literary publishing house. Our books result from artistic collaboration between writers, artists, and editors. Over the years we have become a far-flung community of activists whose energies bring humanitarian enlightenment and hope to individuals and communities grappling with the major issues of our time—peace, justice, the environment, education and gender. This is a humane and highly creative group of people committed to art and social change. The poems, stories, essays, non-fiction explorations of major issues are significant evidence that despite the relentless violence of our time, there is hope and there is art to show the human face of it.

to Jennifer and Robert

Map of Providencia

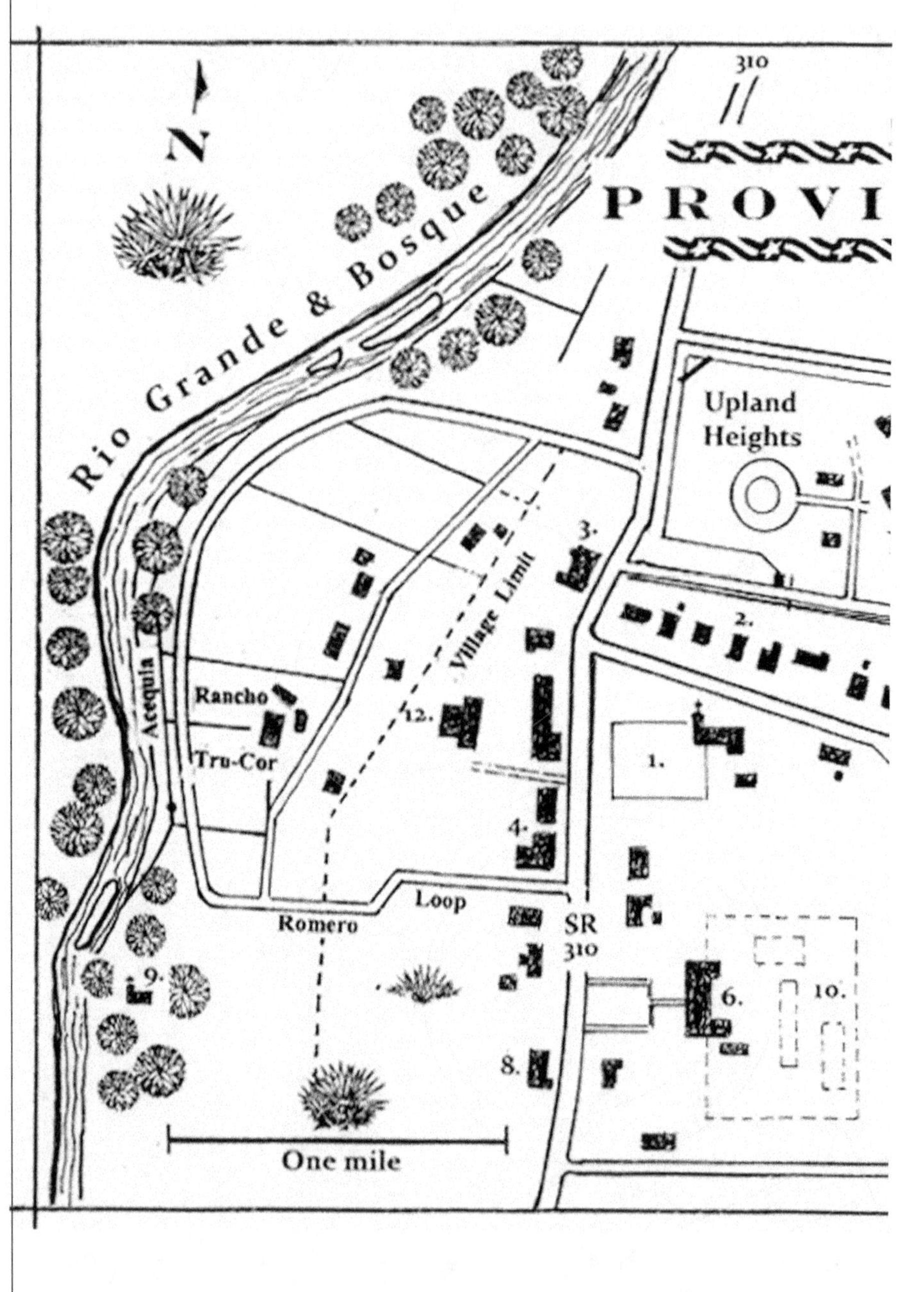

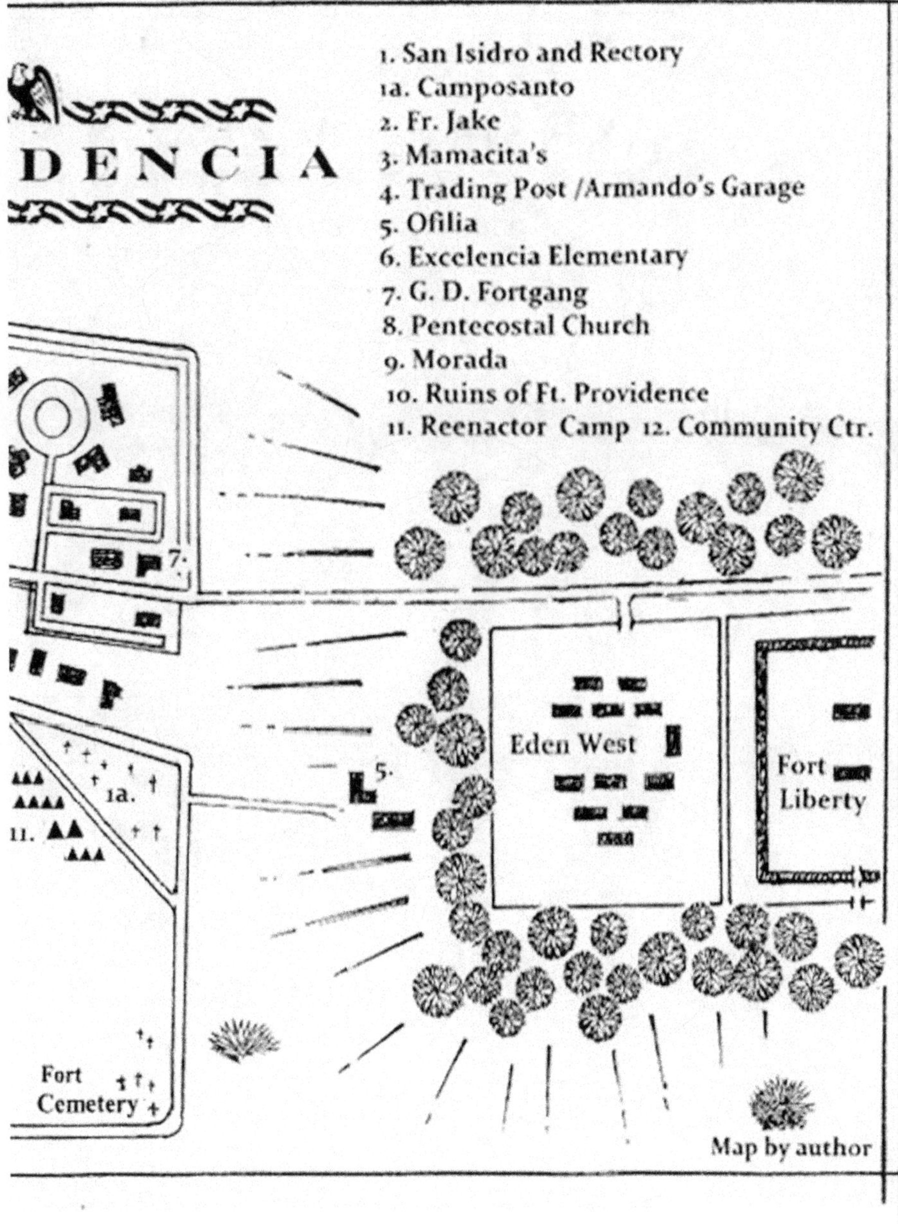

DENCIA
1. San Isidro and Rectory
1a. Camposanto
2. Fr. Jake
3. Mamacita's
4. Trading Post /Armando's Garage
5. Ofilia
6. Excelencia Elementary
7. G. D. Fortgang
8. Pentecostal Church
9. Morada
10. Ruins of Ft. Providence
11. Reenactor Camp 12. Community Ctr.
7.
5.
1a.
11.
Eden West
Fort Liberty
Fort Cemetery
Map by author

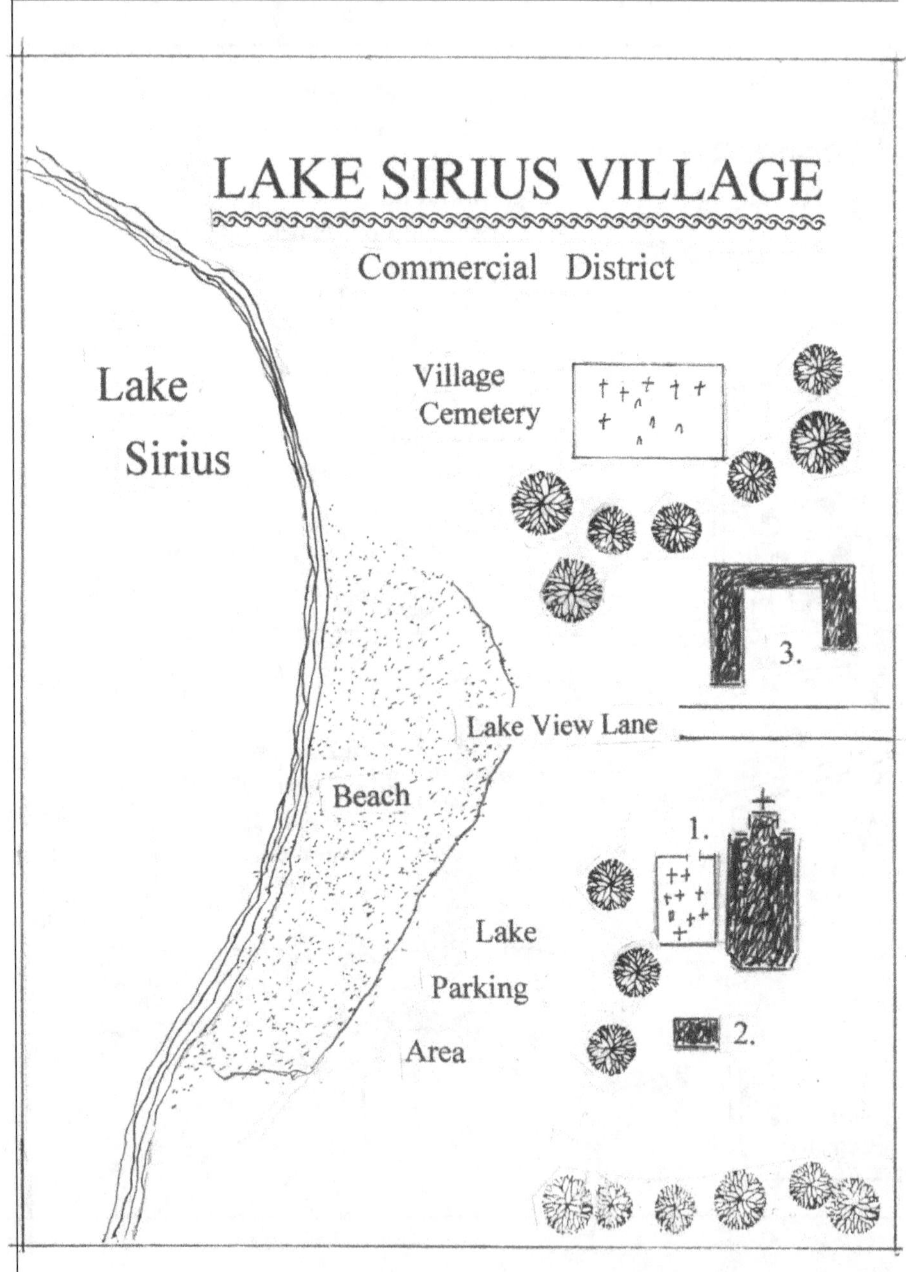
LAKE SIRIUS VILLAGE
Commercial District
Lake
Sirius
Village
Cemetery
3.
Lake View Lane
Beach
1.
Lake
Parking
Area
2.

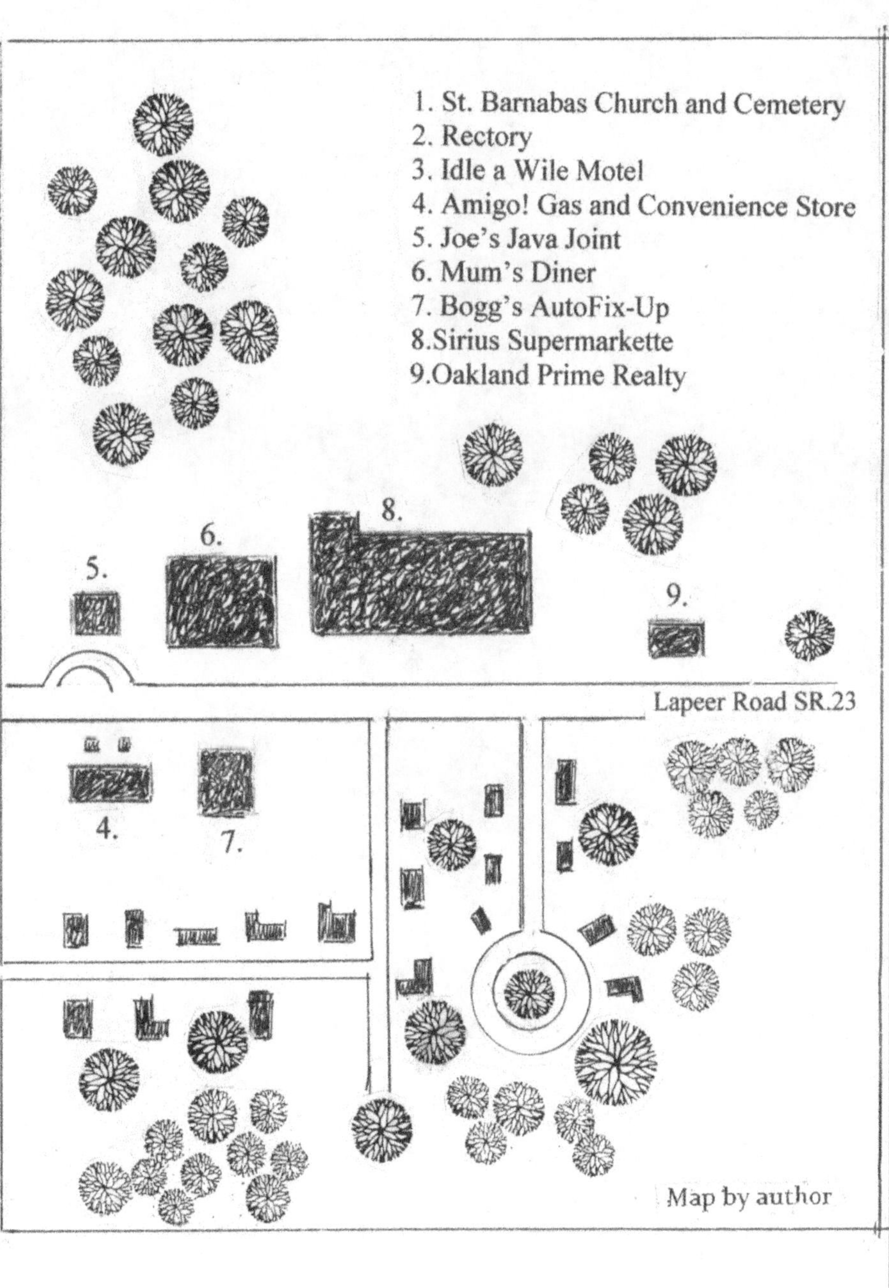

1. St. Barnabas Church and Cemetery
2. Rectory
3. Idle a Wile Motel
4. Amigo! Gas and Convenience Store
5. Joe's Java Joint
6. Mum's Diner
7. Bogg's AutoFix-Up
8.Sirius Supermarkette
9.Oakland Prime Realty
8.
6.
5.
9.
Lapeer Road SR.23
4.
7.
Map by author

1 prologue

As a favor from the Archbishop of Detroit to his colleague, the Archbishop of Santa Fe, 70-year-old Polish priest, Casimir Jakubowski—Fr. Jake—is sent to Providencia, New Mexico, to aid an ill and dysfunctional priest, Father Jésus Mora. Fr. Jake leaves his Michigan parish, St. Barnabas on the Lake, at the small village of Lake Sirius, and flies to New Mexico. Shortly after he arrives, Father Mora, the Pastor at San Isidro Church, is found murdered. His niece, Detective Sonia Mora, is assigned to the case and discovers her uncle was poisoned. Why and by whom? Father Jake is assigned as the priest at San Isidro, yet being an outsider, "*Norteño*," Fr. Jake is not accepted by the Hispanic deacon at the church and is locked out. However, several other members of the congregation befriend and support Fr. Jake. When he finally enters the church, he finds a hopelessly out of date parish in terms of Vatican II reforms that include a lack of Sunday Missals, church bulletins and faith formation classes for children. Fr. Jake corrects these with the help of Cynthia Plow, a teacher at the local Elementary school.

As the days go by a series of unexpected incidents that involve drug smuggling, worthless quit claim deeds on residents' homes, an effort to turn part of Providencia into a Ghost Town in which to film horror movies, Fr. Jake teams up with Detective Mora to help solve the cases.

It is now August 1st. On that day, Fr. Jake receives a call from a former parishioner and friend at his church in Michigan, which will make him return to Lake Sirius and conduct a Memorial Service.

2 an august call from michigan for fr. jake

Sunday, August 1st, in Providencia, New Mexico, dawned hot and muggy. Threatening storm clouds darkened the sky and the rumble of thunder sounded from a distant storm.

In the rectory of San Isidro Church, after a restless sleep, Fr. Casimir Jakubowski awoke early and feeling ill. He suffered from an upset stomach and wondered what he had eaten for supper on the evening before that cause his discomfort.

"I think I'll take a couple of antacid tablets, skip breakfast, and just have coffee," he muttered to himself, then looked out the kitchen window to see if he could watch the oncoming storm. "Monsoons" they were called in New Mexico, which the priest still thought was an unlikely name. *I'll not put out any bird bread today because of rain. I'm still impressed by the intelligence of crows. One, probably a female, seems to recognize me and doesn't fly off when I come out with the bread.* Fr. Jake looked to west toward the Rio Grande bosque. *Misting up. The Spanish explorers that traveled this way picked beautiful locations to begin colonies.* He glanced at his watch. *6:34. I better stop my musings and start brewing that coffee.*

Fr. Jake took down a newly bought can of coffee from a small walnut-stained cabinet above the sink. After he pried off the plastic top with his fingers, he saw a thin aluminum foil covering that protected the contents.

I'll need my Swiss Army knife to cut this foil off, he thought, and found the knife in a drawer. After the priest opened the smallest blade to cut out the foil, he remembered that Al Franzek, a parishioner and friend at his Michigan church, St Barnabas-on-the-Lake, had given him the knife on April 1st as a birthday gift. "Handy little tool the Swiss make in a beautiful little country." Fr. Jake thought a moment before remembering that the first day of August was a significant date for the Swiss. After he set his coffee pot on brew, the priest went to his living room and took an Encyclopedia Britannica off the book shelf and thumbed through to the pages that told about Switzerland's origins.

"I was correct about the date," Fr. Jake mused aloud. "On August 1, 1291, representatives of three Cantons, Uri, Schweiz, and Unterwalden, swore an oath to defend each other against the then Hapsburg rulers of the area. That's where William Tell comes in." He read on to more recent histories. "Universal military conscription and 'Armed Neutrality' kept the Swiss from an invasion in two World Wars.... I think my coffee is ready." He put the Encyclopedia back on the shelf and went into the kitchen to pour himself a cup of the brew.

Fr. Jake took the coffee to his arm chair and opened his Breviary to the Eighteenth Sunday of Ordinary time. His habit was to read aloud the entries to determine if they might have any relevance to what might happen that day.

The first reading was from the book of Isaiah.

"'Thus says the Lord. Oh, come to the water all you who are thirsty, though you have no money come! Buy corn without money and eat and at no cost, wine and milk. Why spend money on what is not bread, your ages on what fails to satisfy? Listen to me and you will have good things to eat and rich food to enjoy.'" *I do feel a little better but all that talk of food isn't making me hungry,* Fr. Jake thought, then read on. "'Pay attention, come to me, listen and your soul will live. With you I will make an everlasting covenant—'"

The phone ringing interrupted him. He picked up the receiver. "Father Jakubowski, San Isidro. How may I help you?"

"Father, this is Al Franzek in Michigan with sad news, I'm afraid."

"Al, I haven't heard from you in ages. What happened?" Fr. Jake asked.

"My wife, Edyth, passed away suddenly from metastatic cancer last night."

"Al, I'm so sorry. Is there any way I can be of any possible help?"

"Father, it's an awful lot to ask, but I was hoping you might be able to fly in and hold a Cremation Memorial Service for our friends and any villagers who knew her. Edyth thought so highly of you."

"And I of her, Al. Of course, I'll come," Fr. Jake assured him. "Do you have another priest at St. Barnabas now?"

"These days one comes only for a Sunday Mass, and not always the same priest. I truly think the Archbishop will close the church. As you'll recall, Father, attendance at Mass is pretty good in the summer, but all those tourists don't come in the winter. It's a matter of dwindling offerings for the upkeep of the church. Even a number of our older people who lived in Lake Sirius when you were here, Catholics who went to Mass, have moved to care homes in Detroit or Oakland County."

"All in a matter of about four months since I arrived in New Mexico," Fr. Jake remarked, then asked, "Al, how do you propose I should come to Michigan?"

"Fly here, Father. I'd buy Southwest Airlines round trip tickets from your Albuquerque airport."

"That would work," Fr. Jake told him, "and I can hitch a ride to the Sunport with a friend here, Armando Herrera."

Franzek asked, "When could you leave, Father?"

"As soon as possible for your sake," he replied. "Tomorrow in the afternoon would be fine."

"How about getting back to New Mexico?"

"In about four days, say August 6."

"Good. I'll Contact Southwest Airlines and call you back today with the flight times."

"I'll be there, Al. Despite the sad occasion, I'm looking forward to seeing you."

"Same here. Good bye for now, Father."

"Good bye, Al. Again, my condolences."

Fr. Jake put down the receiver, took a deep breath, and looked at his watch. *I better get over to the church for the eight o'clock Mass...I barely have time to vest.*

As the priest left the rectory, a loud clap of thunder sounded and it began to rain.

Inside San Isidro, schoolteacher Cynthia Plow was distributing missals in the pews when she saw Fr. Jake come in and greeted him.

"Good morning, Father. I thought I heard rain outside. Did you get wet?"

"A bit, Cynthia, nothing serious," he told her, wiping his hair with a handkerchief.

"A lot of parishioners might wait for the ten o'clock," she said, just as Armando and his Aunt Ofilia came in the front door holding a dripping umbrella.

"Glad you're here Armando," Fr. Jake told him. "I received sad news by phone from a friend in Michigan and may need your help tomorrow afternoon."

"Sure, Father Hakub. What is it?"

"I need to vest for Mass now," the priest said, "so I'll tell you and Cynthia afterward."

❧❧

After Mass, Armando, his *curandera* aunt, and Cynthia waited in the first pew for Fr. Jake to speak to them.

In a few moments he came over to tell the three about his phone call that morning, but Ofilia had the first word. "*Padre*, you don't look too good," she told him, frowning. "You feel sick or something?"

"Auntie…not now," Armando warned.

Fr. Jake held up a hand and winked at him. "It's okay. Ofilia, I did have an upset stomach when I got up, and didn't eat breakfast, but did take an antacid pill."

"Bah, they no good. I got right potion. Mando, bring my tray from car."

"Auntie, it's still raining outside," he protested.

"Use umbrella. Bring tray," she insisted. "Be good boy."

After Armando went out to his Camaro for the tray, Cynthia looked at Fr. Jake and smiled. It was a routine Ofilia followed with friends or strangers. She would find a use for one of her herbs, salves, or potions, and then charge for her help.

When Armando returned, Ofilia selected a small bottle from the tray, opened it, and held it up under Fr. Jake's nose. "You smell, *padre*."

After sniffing the bottle, he asked her, "Mint?"

"Other thing, too," Ofilia said, "You take, you well."

"I'll do that after Mass back at the rectory," he told her. "How much?"

Ofilia held out her hand. "Five dollar, *padre*."

"A bargain," he told the old woman, grinning at her chuzpah, and reached back for his wallet.

Cynthia asked, "Now, Father, can you tell us about that phone call?"

"I wait in car," Ofilia said. "Mando, you bring tray, umbrella, come back in church to listen."

"When Armando returned, Fr. Jake told him and Cynthia, "I wanted to let you know that the wife of a good friend, Al Franzek, back at my old parish in Michigan died. Al asked if I could come and perform a Memorial Service tomorrow. I said I would."

Cynthia wondered, "Father, how will you get there?"

"He's getting an afternoon reservation for me on Southwest Airlines and will call me today."

"When I know the time, Armando, I was wondering if you could drive me to the Sunport?"

"Sure, Father Hakub, be glad to do that."

"How long will you be gone, Father?" Cynthia asked.

"Probably a few days," he told her. "I also may visit my Archbishop, as they're thinking of closing my old church there."

"Who will celebrate Mass at San Isidro while you're way, Father?"

Fr. Jake shrugged. "Cynthia, If I haven't returned by next Sunday, you may have to go to the Mission church Carlotta attends a short way down Highway 10. Ask her where it is."

"Okay, Father, I will," she told him, "but it won't be the same without you."

3 fr. jake prepares to leave for michigan

After Fr. Jake returned to the rectory, he tried Ofilia's 'medication.' After taking a sip, he thought, *Not bad. Minty and it even might help.* He looked at his watch. 9:23. *Plenty of time to get ready for my 10:00 a.m. Mass. After that I'll maybe have a bowl of soup for lunch, then start packing and wait for Al's phone call. It's about a five-hour flight.*

At the ten o'clock Mass, Fr. Jake told a sparse congregation, due to a pouring rain, that he had to travel to Michigan for a few days, yet not the reason. He repeated his advice to Cynthia that if he hadn't returned by next Sunday, they should ask Carlotta about the location of her Mission church on Highway 310.

Around Noon, still feeling a bit queasy, for lunch Fr. Jake opened a can of Campbell condensed chicken rice soup, added only a half can of water, poured it into a saucepan, and set it on the stove to heat up.

While eating, he began to think about the Memorial service he would conduct the next day.

I haven't yet had a funeral at San Isidro, so I should look up funeral prayers in my Breviary. I'll do that after I've eaten this soup.

Finished, he put the empty bowl on the sink and brought his Breviary to the table. After opening it to 'Funeral Mass outside the Easter Season' he read aloud. "'Give Edyth eternal rest, Oh Lord, and may perpetual light shine on her forever. Almighty God, we firmly believe that your Son died and rose to life. We pray for Edyth, who has died in Christ. Raise her at the last day to share the glory of the risen Christ, who lives and reigns forever'—"

The telephone ringing interrupted Fr. Jake's reading. *That could be Al Franzek.* He picked up the receiver. "Father Jakubowski, San Isidro. How may I help you?"

"Father, this is Al with your Round Trip flight information. Do you have a pad and pencil?"

"Right next to me. Go ahead."

"You'll be on Southwest Airlines Flight 245, leaving Albuquerque at 10:30 in the morning and landing at 4:20 in the afternoon at the lower level of Concourse D. You'll see the Southwest gate. I'll wait for you in their lobby."

"Thanks, Al." Fr. Jake replied. "I'll pack a carry-on and ask my friend, Armando, to drop me off at the Southwest Airlines Departures location around 8:30. That should be enough time for me get a boarding pass at the Southwest desk and be on time for the flight."

"Your ticket will be there waiting in your name, Father. Have a safe flight."

"Thanks, Al. God Bless."

Fr. Jake hung up and looked at his watch. *I'll call Armando later today. Now I should start packing and remember to go to the grocery and tell Carlotta I'll be gone for six days. Also buy a frozen Lasagna for dinner this evening.*

After getting his carry-on bag down from a closet shelf, Fr. Jake put in enough underwear, socks and two folded blue shirts to last him for the time he would be away. He tucked in his Breviary and Mass Kit with two San

Isidro wooden *santos*, one for Archbishop Sredzinski, and the other for his secretary, Mrs. Belinski.

The morning rain had let up by the time Fr. Jake left the rectory and walked to Carlotta's grocery, but the heat was still oppressive. When he reached the store the bell tinkled as the priest entered. Carlotta was alone, fanning herself.

"*Buenos tardes*, Padre. How are you doing in this heat?"

"Carlotta, how do you say 'surviving' in Spanish," he asked, grinning.

"*Sobrevivir*," she replied, "and I know what you mean."

"I see you're trying to keep cool."

"And doing a darn poor job of it," she complained. "My sciatica is acting up a bit, lately. Oh, well…. May I get you anything?"

"I came to buy a Lasagna, but mainly to let you know I'm going to Michigan tomorrow and will be gone for at least six days."

"You had to have a good reason, Father, but I guess it'll be cooler up there."

"It's a sad reason, Carlotta," Fr. Jake told her. "The wife of a good friend at my parish died and asked me to perform a Memorial Service."

"You'll fly, of course."

"Yes, a Southwest Airlines flight in the morning. I'll ask Armando to drive me to the Sunport."

She laughed. "With him driving his Camaro, that won't take long at all, Father."

"We'll leave pretty early, 8:30," he said. "Let me get the lasagna."

After Fr. Jake paid for his purchase, Carlotta shook his hand. "Have a good flight, Father."

"Thanks, God bless."

❧❦

At the rectory, Fr. Jake could feel he had perspired on his walk back. He splashed cold water on his face with a wash cloth, dried off, then rang up Armando. The young mechanic readily agreed to drive him, and said he would pick up the priest at the specified 8:30 time.

Fr. Jake cooked and ate his supper, set his alarm clock for 6:00 a.m. and went to bed early.

4 fr. jake leaves new mexico to go to michigan

Thinking about his forthcoming trip kept Fr. Jake from quickly falling asleep. When he finally slept, it was fitful and irregular, with periods of wakefulness in which he felt uneasy about how things would turn out when he reached his old parish at Lake Sirius, after Al Franzek had picked him up at the Detroit Metro Airport.

When Fr. Jake's alarm went off at 6:00 a.m., he had dozed off a short while before. Startled, he reached over to turn it off. *It's light outside*, he thought, *so perhaps I should have a quick breakfast, just the raisin bran, and be dressed and ready to leave when Armando gets here.*

After brushing his teeth and shaving, the priest dressed in a light blue short-sleeve shirt, Roman collar, and dark suit, the clerical outfit that identified him as a clergyman. Most of those people who would interact with the priest in public would address him as "Reverend."

Fr. Jake had finished eating his cereal and rinsed out the bowl when he heard the roar of an automobile engine outside. "Armando's Camaro. He's on time," he said aloud and went to open the front door.

Armando, wearing sunglasses, saw him on the porch. "I ain't late am I, Father Hakub?"

"Exactly on time," he told him, smiling. "Let me bring out my carry-on and lock the rectory."

"When the priest was ready, Armando reached over to push open the passenger door. "Hop in, buckle up, Father. Stow your carry-on in back."

"Thanks." Before getting in the car, Fr. Jake looked at the sky. "Bluer than I'll see in Michigan, and perfect flying weather. There's even a slight breeze."

"Right, Father Hakub, and the rain finally let up, so we'll make good time." Armando gunned the Camaro's engine. "Ready?"

"Just about." Fr. Jake sat in the passenger seat, closed the door, and reached back for the seat belt, then noticed that a rosary he had seen in his first ride in the Camaro still hung from the car's rear view mirror. *A fine Hispanic religious tradition.*

When Armando saw that the priest was secured, he backed out of the driveway and into the street. Turning right, he made another right turn on Highway 310 to reach Interstate 25 at Bélen.

Armando turned on the car's air conditioning, then said, "Father Hakub, we know you're from Michigan but you ain't talked much about it. What's it like?"

"Compared to New Mexico? In two words—'Flat and Green.'" Fr. Jake held up his hand. "No, seriously, Armando, the state is shaped like a mitten, even has an area called the Thumb. Also, it's surrounded by water on three sides and license plates have the nickname 'Great Lakes State.'"

"So you really got to learn how to swim," Armando jested.

"True, and quite young since there are dozens of small lakes where it's safer to swim. As to history, you probably learned in school that New Mexico was explored and settled by Spanish conquistadores. In the case of Michigan, it was the French who came over and claimed New France, what's now called Canada. Here we have Old Town, Albuquerque, dating from 1706. Detroit, near where I lived, was settled in 1701, five years earlier."

"Gee, that's a lot of history to memorize."

Fr. Jake said, "I learned some Spanish like '*Habla Espanol*' in Michigan and New Mexico, but a lot less French in Michigan, just a little '*Parlez vous*'."

"That means the same thing?"

"Yes. And to complicate things, Armando, the British, who had settled further south in New England, went to war with the French in 1763 and won, so Canada became English…." Father Jake looked out the window, then glanced at his watch. "How are we doing?"

"The Sunport's off ramp is right up ahead, Father."

"Great. Head for Departures and I'll get out at the Southwest Airlines Check-in." Fr. Jake touched the mechanic's arm. "I really appreciate this, Armando."

"No *problemo*, Father Hakub," he said. "Let me know what time you get back and I come get you." Armando indicated the back seat with his thumb. "Don't forget your carry-on."

Fr. Jake reached back for the case, then leaned into the front compartment before closing the car door. "You're a real friend, Armando. God bless."

"So long. Have a good trip."

Fr. Jake watched the Camaro pull a way for a moment, then walked inside to the Southwest Airlines counter to get his Boarding passes.

"Good morning, Reverend," a clerk said then checked his computer. "Father Casimir Jakubowski round trip to Detroit Metro. Reverend, here are your Boarding Passes. Go to the left, then up the stairs to Security and Concourse B. Flight 245 is on time."

"Thank you."

"Have a good flight, Reverend."

At the security desk, Fr. Jake showed his Driver's license ID with the boarding passes and was waved through without comment. At the entrance to Concourse B, he bought a burrito and coffee, knowing that in Economy seating no food would be served on the airplane—at best a small bag of cookies or peanuts, and a choice of drinks would be available.

The Southwest Airlines lobby was not crowded. Fr. Jake found a seat with a discarded newspaper dated August 2, sat down and glanced at his watch. *Going on 9:30. About 40 minutes to wait before boarding.* He unwrapped the Burrito, took sip of coffee, then looked at the front page of the paper. Two homicides and three robberies were reported with other non-criminal happenings in Albuquerque. The inside pages told of flooding in Pakistan, due to heavy Monsoon rains, and a side bar about Pope Benedict XVI getting new charges that church leaders had covered up sex crimes against minors by Catholic clergy members.

The article on religion reminded Fr. Jake that he had not read his Breviary that day as he usually did every morning after breakfast. He set aside the newspaper to zip open his carry-on and find the book. Settled back, he read that August 2 commemorated Bishop Eusebius of Vercelli. The Bishop had preached against the Arian heresy which denied the divinity of Christ. Arians caught, tortured and exiled him.

Fr. Jake silently read the Opening Prayer. '*Saint Eusebius affirmed the Divinity of your son. By keeping the faith he taught may we come to share the eternal life of Christ, who lives and reigns with you and the Holy Spirit, one God forever and ever.*

The priest had read through half of the Gospel of John when a loudspeaker announced that passengers for Flight 245 were to prepare to board the plane. Fr. Jake replaced the Breviary in his carry-on and walked over to stand with other passengers. Boarding passes were labeled A, B and C. No seat numbers were assigned—one simply walked down the aisle and chose a seat.

Fr. Jake's pass was a C. When his number was called, he gave his pass to the gate attendant. She smiled at him when he thanked her. At the airplane door, a young African-American stewardess also smiled as she greeted passengers coming onboard. A short way down the narrow aisle, holding his carry-on awkwardly in front of him, he saw that a man had taken the window seat of a three-seat space. Fr. Jake indicated the middle seat and asked, "Sir, is this seat taken?"

"No…Father. Help yourself."

"Thanks." Fr. Jake stowed his carry-on in front of his feet, then clicked on the safety belt, and leaned back to close his eyes.

The man nudged him and extended a hand. "Name's Jim Hutchins, Father. I'm Catholic."

Fr. Jake leaned over to return the handshake. "Father Jakubowski, Jim. A mouthful, I'm afraid."

"Sure is," he agreed and laughed. "Where you heading to?"

"Michigan. I have a parish there," he told him.

"Then what are you doing New Mexico?"

"Long story. My Archbishop—"

Before Fr. Jake could tell Jim a story he didn't really want him to know, the African-American stewardess he had seen at the door stopped from checking seat belts and handed him a small pillow and eye mask. "Reverend, his will make you a bit more comfortable in case you want to sleep."

"Thank you, Miss. I noticed that round brass pin you're wearing with 07 in the center. May I ask what it is?"

"I'm proud of having graduated that year from Central Technical High School. What I learned there helped me decide to become an airline stewardess. I love my job."

"And you're good at it," he told her. "Thanks for the mask and pillow."

"After we takeoff, another stewardess and I will be back with a snack cart and offer you something to drink."

"I look forward to it." Fr. Jake smiled at her again.

When the stewardess moved far enough away, Jim leaned over to whisper, "Father, I didn't know they hired *them*."

"Them? What do you mean?" Fr. Jake asked, yet understood his racist comment.

"Forget it. Hey, Father, I know a real funny joke about flying for the first time. You'll split a gut laughing."

"That doesn't sound too amusing," Fr. Jake remarked.

Jim began anyway. "So this little guy gets on board a plane for the first time and is given a seat next to this big Texan, who asks him, "You fly before?" When the little guy says "No," the Texan looks at him says, "Aw, ain't nothin' to it," then falls asleep. "'Course the little guy gets airsick as soon as the plane takes off and barfs all over the Texan. When the Texan wakes up and sees what happened, he glares down at the little guy, who asks him very meekly, "Feeling any better?"

Fr. Jake didn't laugh and realized it would not be a very unpleasant flight. He put on the eye mask and leaned back to relax. When two Stewardesses returned shortly after with the snack cart, he asked her name. It was Erma, named after her mother. Both attended a Black church in Detroit, Bethel Baptist. Erma gave the priest an extra package of cookies and the tomato juice he ordered. Jim Hutchins waved her off and stared out the window at the ground below.

As the airplane landed at Detroit Metro and the bell rang for passengers to exit, Jim climbed over the priest's knees to get his carry-on from an overhead bin without saying goodbye.

Good riddance, Fr. Jake thought. It was not Christian to think that way, but he was in Michigan and looking forward to seeing Al Franzek again.

At the cabin door exit a Copilot thanked passengers for flying Southwest. Erma was there with him. Fr. Jake wished her luck.

5 fr. jake meets up with al franzek

After the flight landed, Fr. Jake walked along a tunnel to the Terminal Concourse and saw Al Franzek waiting for him when he came out. He set down the carry-on to share a strong embrace with his longtime friend.

Franzek released the priest. "Father, I can't tell you how much I appreciate you coming out to conduct a Memorial service for my wife."

"Poor Edyth. You said it was cancer. Did she suffer very long?"

"No, my wife passed away at home, in my arms and in the Lord." After a brief pause to wipe away a tear, Franzek asked the inevitable question. "Father, how was your Flight?"

"Tolerable," he replied. "I met an 'interesting' passenger and an African-American Stewardess named Erma, who graduated from a High School in Detroit. She wasn't Catholic but made me feel at home."

"They're trained to do that," Franzek said. "By the way, you look good, Father, and that's a nice New Mexico tan you have." He glanced at his watch. "It's after two o'clock now and it'll take at least an hour to reach Lake Sirius. I'm parked just over there."

The automobile was a 2008 Cadillac Escalade. Franzek wore a white shirt, tan slacks, and a light summer suit jacket. *Al must be doing quite well as an attorney*, Fr. Jake thought.

After both were buckled in the car, and the carry-on stowed on the back seat, Fr. Jake asked, "How's your firm doing these days?"

"Father, there are people who will always get into legal trouble or want to sue someone." Franzek pulled out a business card from his shirt pocket, and handed it to the priest.

"'Franzek, Salazar, and Meidner, Counselors'" Fr. Jake read aloud. "The pretty much covers the ethnicity out here—Polish, Hispanic and German."

"Walter Meidner has an interesting background," Franzek said as he backed his Cadillac out of the parking space and headed toward I-94.

"Interesting in what way?" Jake asked.

"You remember, Father, that during World War Two there was a German POW holding compound a few miles north of Pontiac, Camp Juno, it was called, and Walter's father, Hans, was held there. After interrogating him, the authorities determined that he wasn't a Nazi fanatic who worshipped Hitler, just a drafted Wehrmacht soldier doing his duty to the Fatherland. I've been to do some research on the Camps."

"Interesting so far," Fr. Jake told him. "Go on, Al."

"It may sound unbelievable, but there were 6,000 POWs interned in 32 camps Michigan. It's ironic, Father, but they may have helped us win the war."

"How so?"

"There was a labor shortage in this country because of the wartime draft, so prisoners were allowed to work on farms, growing crops, pulping wood and so on. They even were paid 81 cents a day."

"Al," Fr. Jake asked, "how does this all tie in with Walter Meidner being in your firm?"

"Obviously, after the war was over, most of the POWs went back to Germany in 1945. Hans didn't. He applied for American citizenship, got it five years later, and eventually married a woman of German descent."

"That would be Walter's mother."

"Exactly, Father."

Franzek drove in silence until they reached the off ramp to I-75.

"Remember, we take I-75 left to Pontiac then Highway 24 to Lake Sirius."

"Al, "Fr. Jake told him, "I've never driven this far south, only as far as the Chancellery Building, when I was interviewed by Archbishop Sredzinski and sent to New Mexico to help a dysfunctional priest Father Jésus Mora."

"I remember. How did that work out? You've never told much me much about your time while there."

"Sorry, Al, I should have written. I didn't know what to expect at Providencia, the village where the Father Mora's Church of San Isidro is located. New Mexico's slogan, I guess you'd call it, is 'The Land of Enchantment' yet it was anything but that."

"Seriously? In what way?"

"Al, Father Mora was dysfunctional, but also senile, bordering on dementia. The priest had heard about me, but was hostile, and accused me of coming there to take over his church."

"Not the reception you expected."

"Of course not. Also a deacon at the church resented me as an outsider, worse a Norteño who wasn't even Hispanic." Fr. Jake paused, wondering how much to tell his friend. "Al, the climax of what happened was in a *Sagrario*, a chapel Father Mora built at one side of the church to display the Blessed Sacrament, large host, in a Monstrance. The priest was found murdered there and the host missing. Father Mora's niece, Sonia Mora, a detective with a local Sheriff's Department, was assigned to the case. I worked with Sonia to solve her uncle's murder, and we became good friends."

"That's quite a story, Father." Franzek held his Cadillac to the speed limit and had reached the intersection with Highway 24. He slowed down to observe the road's 35 mile limit. "Almost to Lake Sirius, about 20 miles yet to go. We'll have dinner at Mum's Diner and talk some more."

"Sounds good, I didn't have much to eat for lunch." Fr. Jake sat back to relax. *How will the village look after my four months away?*

A sign placed the Village of Lake Orion 10 miles off. At Oxford, Franzek turned right; Lake Sirius was 3 miles distant.

At the sign Fr. Jake said, "Al, I've only left Lake Sirius once before and there can't be many changes since I went to New Mexico five months ago."

Franzek slowed the car to 30 miles an hour. "Probably not, Father. There's Oakland Prime Realty up ahead still boarded up. I told you more elderly people are leaving here and younger ones aren't buying property."

"Sirius Supermarkette still sells groceries," Fr. Jake noted.

"All year, Father, but prices go up in the winter, after all the tourists leave."

"Bogg's Auto Fix is closed."

"Christian goes home at Five," Franzek explained. "Not enough residents need repairs and the families who come to fish and swim have their own auto shops where they live." He pointed to the right. "Mum's Diner, where we'll eat. She'll stop serving customers at Nine, but we'll have plenty of time to order."

Joe's Java Joint was not open. When Fr. Jake saw Amigo! Gas and Convenience Store, he recalled that it closed at 10:00 p.m. Idle-a-Wile Motel flashed a red neon VACANCY sign.

At the St. Barnabas-on-the-Lake Catholic Church sign, Franzek pulled into the church's gravel parking lot and turned off the ignition.

"Home safely, Father."

"And the church doesn't look abandoned, Al," Fr. Jake remarked in a half jest.

"I told you a priest will come, and not always the same one, to at least celebrate a Sunday Mass. Incidentally, while you are here, you could sleep at our…I mean…my place."

"Thanks, Al." *Remembering Edyth.* First let me look inside the rectory. I probably won't have to do much other than sweep out a few mice droppings."

"As you wish…" Franzek looked at the clock on the Cadillac's dashboard. "Why don't I come over at seven? We could walk to Mum's Diner, it's almost still light outside at nine o'clock."

"Good plan." Fr. Jake opened the car door. "I'll take my carry-on and freshen up a bit until Seven."

"I should do the same," Franzek replied. "See you then."

Fr. Jake, made a Sign of the Cross facing the church, then walked to the rectory, *Might be three month's worth of mice droppings by now,* the priest thought, walking up the rectory stairs. It, too, was locked but Fr. Jake had hidden a key under the eaves and used it open the door.

Indeed, a rush of fetid air almost made the priest gag. Fr. Jake left the door ajar and cranked open a steel-framed window to let an evening breeze help dispel the foul odor of more than a 'few mouse droppings'.

"I've lived here for ten years and had forgotten how large this is rectory compared to the one at San Isidro," he said aloud. "Even has a TV and upper second bedroom for anyone who stays the night." He laid his carry-on valise on the bed and went to his bathroom to shave. Afterward he anticipated that at dinner Al Franzek would talk about the next day's Memorial Service.

How many would attend? Many who knew Edyth would not be Catholic, but would be there.

Fr. Jake glanced at his watch. "I have time to go over the details of a Funeral Mass before Al comes over and I will recite aloud the Prayers for the Dead." He opened his Breviary and read, "'Give Edyth eternal rest, O Lord and may perpetual light shine on her forever. God, you have called your daughter Edyth from this life. Father of all mercy, fulfill her faith and hope in you and lead her safely home to heaven, to be happy with you forever.'"

Al Franzek was on time. Mum's Diner was not crowded, but several residents of Lake Sirius saw Fr. Jake come in and hurried over to greet him. One asked if he was to be their pastor again or would he go back to New Mexico? Evidentially not everyone in the village knew Edyth or had heard of her death.

Ron, one of Mum's sons who ran the restaurant, rapped on a table for attention. "Father came here to hold a Memorial Service for Edyth Franzek tomorrow. Mister Franzek is with him. Father, can you give us some of the details, please?"

Father Jake stood up to say, "Thank you Ron. Edyth has been cremated, so an urn of her ashes will be placed on a small table in front of the altar. Mass will be at 10 a.m. Any questions?"

There were none so Fr. Jake sat down. Franzek signaled to Ron for a menu, then asked the priest. "Father, had you eaten here before?"

"Not that I recall,"

"The specialty is fish, of course, but the meat loaf is my preference," Franzek said. "Doesn't go well with wine but how about a cold beer?"

"Ron, please make that two of the same," Fr. Jake said, eyebrows raised.

"Coming right up." he replied, taking back the menu.

While they waited, Franzek asked, "Father, you've been pastor here for a decade. At what other Michigan churches did you serve?"

"Well, at first as Assistant Pastor," Fr. Jake recalled. "Since I came from Poland and was ordained at Saint's Cyril and Methodius Seminary, and didn't know Michigan that well, the Archbishop kept me close to home, as it were. Let's see…. Churches in Rochester, Troy…Farmington Hills. Livonia may have been the furthest. Pastors were kept only about ten years at any one parish."

Franzek counted on his fingers. "So about four and—"

Ron bringing their meals and drinks interrupted him.

"Looks delicious," Fr. Jake commented.

The waiter bowed slightly, "*Bon apetit.* Enjoy your dinner."

After he and Al had eaten a bit, and knowing the Memorial Service was on his friend's mind, Fr. Jake asked, "Where had you intended Edyth's ashes to be interred?"

"The church's cemetery, of course," he replied without hesitating.

"Al, I'm quite sure the Archbishop will close down St. Barnabas," Fr. Jake said. "In that case, memorial stones like Edyth's could be vandalized. Those in the Sirius village cemetery won't be and you visit and bring flowers there."

Franzek put down his knife. "I…I hadn't thought that far ahead."

"It's possible that Edyth's funeral could be the last one at St. Barnabas," Fr. Jake told him. "I must make a courtesy call on Archbishop Sredzinski, at the Chancery Building in Detroit. Since you'll have to drive me, Al, I want you to meet him. There's no doubt in my mind that he will close, or worse, sell the church building."

Ron noticed that the men had finished eating and came to ask if they wanted dessert. Neither did, and Al asked him to bring the bill.

While they waited, Fr. Jake commented, "It's still light out. Why don't we go to the village cemetery, Al, and find a nice resting place for Edyth tomorrow?"

"Father, I very much like your idea."

Franzek paid the bill and left a tip. Outside, the setting summer sun bathed everything in a reddish glow. The cemetery bordered Lake Sirius and was screened from the village itself by a grove of elm and poplar trees. Fr. Jake stood back while Al walked around the available burial space. He stopped at an area near the water, to ask, "Father, how about here? I'll plant a smaller tree, alongside my wife's Memorial Stone."

"Fine." Fr. Jake agreed. "That will be a good location and you can bring flowers. Tomorrow, we'll have the funeral Mass at St. Barnabas and then proceed to here with the cremation urn and final blessing. I might even be able to find one of my altar boys and have incense."

Franzek turned to give Fr. Jake a tearful hug of gratitude.

At 10:00 a.m. the next morning, pews at St. Barnabas were crowded with villagers who came to pay their respects to Al Franzek, a villager almost

everyone knew. Fr. Jake purposely wore a white, not purple chasuble: it was not a joyous occasion but Edyth was with her Lord.

The urn holding Edyth's cremation ashes was set on a small table in front of the altar.

Fr. Jake had found an altar boy, Hugo, who was not at summer camp or vacationing with his parents. With the tinkle of a small bell that announced the beginning of Mass, the congregation stood. Fr. Jake came out of the vestry, with Hugo alongside the priest holding a silver container of incense grains, and swinging a smoking censor on a chain.

At the cremation urn, Fr. Jake added incense, then took the censor from Hugo to incense the urn. He gave the censor back to Hugo and both returned to face the altar and begin Mass with the sign of the cross.

Fr. Jake prayed aloud, "In the name of the Father, and of the Son, and of the Holy Spirit."

In unison the congregation crossed themselves to respond, "Amen."

"The grace and peace of God our Father and the Lord Jesus Christ be with you all,"

"And also with you."

Fr. Jake turned to tell the congregation, "At the end of Mass, Mister Franzek will carry the cremation urn to the burial site and we will proceed there with him for the interment."

❧❦

After Mass ended, not everyone followed Fr. Jake and Franzek to the burial site. The priest incensed the urn and recited a simple prayer over it.

"God, you have called Edyth from this life. Father of all mercy, fulfill her hope and faith in you, and lead her safely home to heaven, to be happy with you forever."

Al Franzek thanked those present and invited them to a simple lunch at Mum's Diner.

It was there that Al reminded Fr. Jake that he wanted to speak with Archbishop Sredzinski at the Chancery and offered to take him there the next day.

6 fr. jake visits his archbishop

That afternoon, by telephone, Fr. Jake confirmed an appointment with Archbishop Stanley Sredzinsky at the Chancery for 2:00 p.m. the next day, Thursday, August 5. The priest called Al Franzek about the time: it would take about an hour to get there so they could leave Lake Sirius at one o'clock.

Fr. Jake ate an early supper at Mum's diner—fish this time—then returned to the rectory.

Curious about what his Breviary might predict for his meeting with the Archbishop, he settled comfortably in his armchair and turned to the August date.

"Hmm," he read aloud, "Dedication of St. Mary Major. After the dogma of the divine Maternity of the Blessed Virgin was declared at the Council of Ephesus, in 431, Pope Sixtus III dedicated this Basilica at Rome in honor of the Mother of God. Later it was called 'St. Mary Major,' the oldest church in the West dedicated to the Blessed Virgin. That could vaguely tie in with the selling of St. Barnabas by the Archbishop and the church being renamed by a new owner."

Fr. Jake read the first part of the Mass Opening Prayer to himself. *Lord, pardon the sins of your people. May the prayers of Mary, the mother of your Son, help to save us, for by ourselves we cannot please you.*

The priest put aside the book and went to check his carry-on valise. With his clothing, he had included two wooden *santos*, hand-carved statues of San Isidro, patron of his church in New Mexico. One was for the Archbishop; the other for his Secretary, Mrs. Belinski. He would suggest they might like to make an *altarcito* shrine, as Ofilia had done for him, where they could have prayers answered. His Excellency might consider that to be a superstition, but it was a widespread Hispanic custom.

Tired from officiating at the Day's Memorial Service, Fr. Jake went to bed early. He would have half the next day to clean up the rectory and church if there actually was a new owner.

∾

In the morning the priest found a half-full box of raisin bran and a somewhat over-ripe banana and breakfasted on that and coffee. He washed the dish and cup, then put on denim work clothes and went outdoors to pull weeds and clip grass around the church perimeter. *Tree branches? I'll just pile them together on one side of the church cemetery.*

After Fr. Jake figured his outdoor work looked decent enough, he went in to make his bed, dust the rectory rooms and make a final effort to sweep up mouse droppings

Once he had finished those tasks, the priest shed his denim clothes to put on dark trousers, his short-sleeved blue shirt and clerical collar, then strolled over to Mum's Diner for a ham sandwich and soft drink. Al Franzek had not come to the rectory, but Fr. Jake guessed he was at the site of Edyth's burial. The priest finished his lunch, paid, then walked back to lock the rectory and wait on his porch with his carry-on valise for Al to arrive.

Franzek's Cadillac pulled up exactly on time.

Fr. Jake came down to open the passenger door and get inside.

"How are you feeling today, Al?" he asked.

"I didn't sleep too well," he admitted.

"Understandable," Fr. Jake said, then put his valise on the back seat.

As Franzek turned the car around to head south, he commented, "It's early Thursday afternoon so traffic shouldn't be too bad. We'll be on time."

"I had a little trouble parking near the Chancery Building the time I went," Fr. Jake said, "but the Archbishop probably hasn't made other appointments."

"Father, I'm looking forward to meeting him," Franzek said. "I've never seen an Archbishop outside of a church service and certainly never spoken with one."

Fr. Jake smiled. "His Excellency is quite human and you'll like him. His business is with me and I'm not that certain about how it will turn out."

❧

Al Franzek was quiet on the drive into Detroit, still remembering the burial of his wife.

Fr. Jake recalled his first visit to the Chancery Building on Washington Boulevard and the somewhat difficult route in reaching the site.

"Al," he said, nudging him, "We're approaching the entrance ramp to I-75. Turn onto that."

"Sorry, Father," he apologized. "I…I better concentrate on driving."

"We're a little more than a half hour from the Chancery," Fr. Jake told him. "No apology needed, but let's hope we get lucky and can park nearby. The Archbishop's office is on the third floor."

Their luck held as Franzek swung his Chrysler into an empty parking space on the Chancery side of the Boulevard. Fr. Jake took his carry-on valise from the back seat. Franzek locked the car, and they walked across the street to take the elevator to Archbishop Sredzinski's office.

Mrs. Belinski was at her desk and glanced at her watch when the two men entered.

"Father Jakubowski, you're right on time," she said in English, probably uncertain if his companion understood Polish or not.

"A pleasure to see you again," Fr. Jake told her. Mrs. Belinski, may I introduce Mister Franzek, a longtime friend of mine. Sadly, I came to Michigan because his wife, Edyth, died and I held a Memorial Service for her burial."

"I'm sorry for your loss, Sir," she sympathized, half standing to touch his hand.

"Thank you…"

"Mrs, Belinski, I brought something for you and His Excellency from New Mexico." Fr. Jake opened his carry-on and took out the carved wooden statue of San Isidro and the candle. "Set up, it's an '*Altarcito*' a Hispanic word meaning something like a home altar. That statue is of San Isidro, the name of my church there."

"*Dobrze.*" she accepted the gift in Polish. "I'll summon...."

Archbishop Sredzinski had heard voices outside his office and expected Fr. Jake, so he opened the door himself. "Kazimieriz Jakubowski, how kind of you to pay me a visit."

When he glanced at his companion, Fr. Jake explained, "Excellency, this is Mister Franzek, a partner with a law firm in Pontiac, but living at Lake Sirius—"

"A lawyer?" The Prelate shook Franzek's hand before Fr. Jake could tell him about Edyth's death. "Come in, come in. I may have work for you—."

"Excellency," Fr. Jake interrupted. "Mister Franzek's wife died and I came to Lake Sirius to conduct a Memorial Service."

The Archbishop crossed himself murmuring, "May she rest in the arms of the Lord."

Fr. Jake set down his carry-on, all thought of telling the Prelate about San Isidro and an *altarcito* evaporating like morning mist.

Archbishop Sredzinski adjusted his glasses and sat behind his mahogany desk. "Please, sit in those armchairs. First, Father Kazimieriz, you'll not return to St. Barnabas. You'll receive retirement pay and could live in a home for retired priests, celebrate Mass, etcetera." He looked toward Franzek. "I sold the St. Barnabas church and rectory to an evangelical group named 'Friends of Jehovah.' Could you handle the paperwork?"

"That's a strange name and wouldn't attract Catholics or Protestants in the community," Fr. Jake commented. "Hopefully, Excellency, they aren't involved in distributing narcotics or some such illegal activity."

Archbishop Sredzinski frowned. "I doubt that's true, Father Kazimieriz."

Franzek said, "Archbishop, I'll do some research about the name before I do any paperwork on the sale and get back to you."

"That does seem prudent," the Archbishop agreed, standing up. "If there's nothing else, I have a three o'clock appointment."

Fr. Jake picked up his carry-on. "Excellency, I had brought you and Mrs. Belinski a wooden statue of San Isidro and instructions for making an *Altarcito* in her home and your rectory. She can explain how to do that."

"Thank you." Archbishop Sredzinski shook hands with Franzek and Fr. Jake, then placed a hand on each man's head and murmured a blessing.

Outside the office, Fr. Jake explained to Mrs. Belinski about the *altarcito* and left the statue of San Isidro and candle with her.

On the elevator back to the car, Franzek scoffed, "A priest's retirement home, Father? I could find you a place to rent in Pontiac. What do you intend to do with your 'free time'?"

"Al," he replied, "I can occasionally fill in for a priest that's on vacation, but am planning an Anti-Hate Center…keeping track of Neo-Nazi individuals or other groups that attempt to undermine this country and expose them. I'm now in touch with an organization that has been doing that, and hope to help them."

"Commendable, Father," he said. "Our law firm has been involved in a few such wrongful defamation lawsuits."

On the drive back to Lake Sirius Franzek asked, "Father, you have your Southwest Airlines Round Trip ticket Boarding Pass for returning to New Mexico on August 6?"

"Al, I do, and thanks again."

"No, I thank you. Do you happen to recall at what time the plane takes off?"

"Yes," Fr. Jake replied. "Southwest Airlines Flight 245 leaves at 9:30 a.m."

Franzek mentally calculated, "So I should get you to Terminal Concourse D at Detroit Metro by eight-thirty and leave here around an hour before that."

"It's about a six hour flight," Fr. Jake recalled, "so I should call Armando and ask him to be at Arrivals by 2:30 p.m."

"Father, do you know how long you'll be in New Mexico before coming back to Michigan?"

"Al, I have unfinished business there," Fr. Jake said, "but it's quite obvious the Archbishop wants me in Michigan. Providencia will need a replacement priest at San Isidro church and I haven't been told of one."

"I just thought of something else," Franzek recalled. "At the Archbishop's I said I could rent you a room. The Catholic Church closest to where I live in Pontiac is St. Andrew's. The priest there is Father Patrick Finnegan and the old rectory has vacant rooms. If you think a Pole could get along with an Irishman, I'll ask Father Finnegan about letting you use one."

Fr. Jake laughed. "If he doesn't have an assistant priest, I could celebrate his Masses when he vacations in Ireland."

"That should convince him."

When Al Franzek and Fr. Jake reached Lake Sirius they ate supper at Mum's Diner. The priest called Armando, who agreed to drive him back to Providencia, and went to bed early.

❧❧

For the Flight back, Fr. Jake wore dark slacks, a short sleeve blue shirt and Roman Collar. Both he and Al Franzek drove to the airport in relative silence, pondering the events of the last few days, and how long it might be before the priest would return to Michigan for good.

❧❧

The Southwest Airlines flight was uneventful, compared to the one that went to Michigan, but Cynthia, not Armando, met Fr. Jake at Arrivals.

After exchanging hugs, on the walk to the parking area, she explained, "Father, Mando had to finish an unexpected repair job and asked me to go the Sunport in his place and drive you back to Providencia."

"For which I thank you, Cynthia," Fr. Jake told her.

Once on the road, Cynthia asked, "How was Michigan?"

"A sad occasion as you realize, but we did resolve a few things in my future, when I finally go back and stay there."

"When will that be?"

"Cynthia, that's up to my Archbishop in Michigan and Archbishop Benisek here, who must find a replacement priest for San Isidro." When he heard her sniffle, Fr. Jake said, "When your school is let out in summer, Cynthia, you can visit and relax. Lake Sirius is quite beautiful."

"Thanks." She drove on in silence and dropped the priest off at his Rectory.

7 carlotta's store is sold

Fr. Jake had been gone six full days. On the next morning after his arrival, August 7, he heard the rumble of distant thunder, and stepped out onto the front porch of the rectory to scan the sky. Massed dark clouds on the horizon foretold rain. "The monsoon season is in full swing," he mumbled to himself. "It probably will be raining by the time I get to the store, so I should bring an umbrella."

He went back inside, where he finished his raisin bran and banana breakfast and cup of coffee, then brought the dish and cup to rinse out in the sink. He already had scattered cut-up "bird bread" in the back yard. A crow on a wire stayed in place, recognizing the priest and by now accustomed to his "daily donation." After breakfast, Fr. Jake would open his breviary to read entries and celebrate what he termed his daily "Kitchen Mass."

∾

For the next twelve days Fr. Jake followed the routine in Providencia he had done before going to Michigan.

≈≈≈

It was now Thursday, August 19. Settled in an armchair, he opened his Breviary to the Twentieth Week of Ordinary Time, thinking, *Let's see if any of the readings give me a hint of what I could, should or might do today.* The First Reading was from the Book of Judges.

"The spirit of the Lord came on Jephthah," he read aloud, a habit he had acquired, since being celibate was a lonely vocation, "who crossed Gilead and Manasseh, passed through to Mizpah in Gilead and from Mizpah in Gilead made his way to the rear of the Ammonites. And Jephthah made a vow to the Lord, 'if you deliver the Ammonites into my hands, then the first person to meet me from the door shall belong to the Lord, and I will offer him up as a holocaust.'" *No, a bit too bloody,* he thought and turned the page. *Move on to the Responsorial Psalm.* "' Here I am Lord. I come to do your will.' Good, that's more like it. 'Happy the man who has placed his trust in the Lord and has not gone over to the rebels who follow false gods. You do not ask for sacrifice and offerings but an open ear. You do not ask for holocaust and victim. Instead here am I.'"

Fr. Jake closed the book and stood up. *Not sure how an open ear applies to me,* he thought, *but I better get to ready celebrate my daily eight o'clock Mass. Not many people attend, mostly the retired elderly, and even fewer today because of the rain. After that I'll go over to Carlotta's and see what I might buy for dinner. I've had just about everything she has that's frozen. I'll kid her a bit about not having Polska Kielbasa, a sausage I can cook."*

≈≈≈

The grocery was short a short walk south down Highway 10 where Fr. Jake lived. Along the way behind Western Savings, where a small bank in a double-wide manufactured home shared space with the Providencia post office, he noticed that a new looking white building was still unoccupied. *I had suggested that might become a community center. Provenceños, young and old, might use it as a recreational center, but nothing yet has been done.*

The Carlotta Ulibarri's grocery had two gasoline pumps in front and a shop in the rear where Armando Herrera repaired cars. *I wonder how Armando is doing, and his curandera aunt, Ofilia. They've become good friends with me.*

Fr. Jake half smiled at a familiar sign in the front window: "The small store with the big heart." A small bell tinkled as he entered. Carlotta sat behind the counter at the cash register. As usual, she greeted the priest in Spanish to help him learn the language.

"*Buenos…dias, Padre.*"

"*Buenos dias,* Carlotta," he replied in turn.

"Father, you're a bit later than usual."

"Wrestling with an Old Testament verse in my Breviary."

The store was empty except for a dark-haired, somewhat swarthy man at the far end of one of the three side aisles. Fr. Jake nodded to him, then paused a moment before asking, "Carlotta you seem nervous this morning. Are you well?"

"Father, my sciatica is acting up somethin' fierce. Awful pain shootin' down my leg. I've decided to go live with my sister in La Fonda. Also she was just diagnosed with a lump on her left breast that might be cancerous."

"I'm so sorry. Who is your sister's doctor? Could I help get both of you to a treatment Center?"

"Thanks, Father, we'll make out."

"When you leave who will run this store?"

"Father, that gentleman over there is Mister Ahmed. I…I've sold the store to him. He'll take over on September first."

8 son of the Imam

Fr. Jake went over to shake the new owner's hand. "Welcome to Providencia, Mister Ahmed. I'm Father Jakubowski, the Catholic priest at St. Isidro Church here. How in the world did you find out about Carlotta's grocery?"

"Thank you Pastor," Ahmed replied. "As you probably suspected, I'm Muslim. My father is the Imam at the Islamic Center of New Mexico in Albuquerque."

"Imam?" Fr. Jake asked. "I'm not familiar with the term. What sort of clerical work does he do?"

"It's a leadership position, perhaps like your bishops but without ordained priests as in Christian churches. Muslims go to a Mosque to pray and do so five times a day."

"If I'm not being too intrusive, tell me why you bought Carlotta's grocery? No, wait, I'd like to know more about you and your family. I'll tell my congregation."

"That would be helpful, Pastor. I'm sure there could be some resentment at the sale."

"Possibly, Mister Ahmed," Fr. Jake said, "let me suggest that we go talk at Mamacita's. It's a restaurant close to where I live."

"I've already had breakfast, Pastor."

"Then just for coffee. Please. I'd like to know more both about you and your religion. I'd read it's the second largest in the world after Christianity."

Ahmed nodded, but thought a moment before agreeing. "I…I could drive us up there. My car is here."

"Good."

"*Bueno*, but, call me Bahir, my first name, not Mister."

"Fine, and I see you know some Spanish. Fr. Jake signaled to Carlotta. "Thanks, we'll be leaving now."

"I heard," she told him. "Glad you both are getting along. *Hasta*."

Buckled inside a black 2008 Chevrolet Impala, the two men drove a mile to Mamacita's and parked outside. At this hour on a Thursday, the restaurant was not crowded. Julia, the young waitress, saw Fr. Jake and an unfamiliar man come inside with him. She beckoned them to a side table.

"'Morning Father. We're running low on *Huevos Rancheros* but I probably could rustle up enough for both of you."

Fr. Jake introduced his companion. "Julia, this is Mister Ahmed."

"Welcome to Mamacita's, sir."

"Thank you, Miss."

"Julia, both of us have eaten breakfast so just some coffee, please. We'd like to stay awhile and talk, if that's okay."

"Sure thing, Father. I'll bring your coffee."

Ahmed looked around a moment then commented, "Nice cozy place."

"My 'Getaway'" Fr. Jake quipped. "Mind if I ask you a few background questions, Bahir?"

"Of course not, Pastor, go ahead."

"How did you discover Carlotta's store?"

"Well, I was born in New Mexico, liked it, and wanted to learn more about the state. I'd heard about the El Camino Real International Heritage Center on I-25 and when I drove down to see it with my wife and kids, stopped for gas at Carlotta's."

"You're married then—"

Julia arrived with the coffee. "Sugar and creamer," she offered. "Let me know if you need anything else."

"Thanks, Julia."

Both took a sip while the beverage was hot, then Bahir said, "You asked if I was married. I am. My wife is Amira and we have a twelve-year-old boy, Galib, and an eight-year-old daughter, Dalia."

"You told me your father was an Imam at the Islamic Center in Albuquerque. Ah…do you get along with him?"

"Well, he wants me to study the Koran, beginning to end, and someday succeed him. His health isn't that great. I know I'd find that vocation… his job…confining."

"What exactly does your father do?" Fr. Jake asked.

"Actually quite a bit…religious classes, social help where needed. Daily services. A Friday prayer and sermon we call *Jum'ah salat*. It's confining to me, if that's the correct word, because it's the same routine every week, same people. Pastor, owning a store where residents buy groceries assures that I'll eventually meet everyone in Providencia, and it seems the village is growing."

"That makes sense," Fr. Jake said, then asked. "Where exactly is this Islamic Center?"

"On Yale Boulevard Southeast, about an 80-mile round trip from Providencia."

"So you'd have to move here with your family?"

"True, perhaps to a place in that Upland Heights Estates subdivision."

When the restaurant door abruptly opened, Fr. Jake looked over to see Armando Herrera and his aunt Ofilia come in, glance around, then head for their table. Ofilia followed behind him, wearing a colorful scarf and skirt and carrying her wooden platter of curative herbs and ointments.

"Hi, Father Hakub." Armando said in greeting. "Carlotta told me you were here with that new store owner."

"Yes, let me introduce him. "Mister Ahmed, this is Armando who runs the auto repair service behind the grocery. Ofilia is his aunt. She's a *curandera*."

Puzzled, Ahmed said, "I don't understand that Spanish word, *curandera*."

Fr. Jake told him, "It describes a woman folk healer and—" But before Fr. Jake could explain further, Ofilia had tugged up Ahmed's sleeve. "You got hurt arm, Mister? Rash maybe? I have cure. You, *Padre* Hakub. How you skin now?"

"All better, *Gracias*—"

"Auntie," Armando broke in with a mild protest. "Don't bother Mister Ahmed right now. We gotta know more about him." He turned to ask, "I hear you're an Ayrab."

"Arab," he corrected, "and I'm also called a Muslim because of my religion. Do you know much about Islam?"

"Naw, never had to."

"The word means 'Submission to God'. We worship in a mosque, and pray five times a day."

"Armando," Fr. Jake said, "I'm sure Cynthia can talk to Mister Ahmed about Islam, perhaps borrow a Koran and give a class about the religion the villagers could attend."

"Still," Armando insisted, "you're not real Americans."

"I was born in Albuquerque. My father has naturalization papers and is an American citizen."

Fr. Jake was surprised at a possible streak of prejudice he hadn't realized was in his friend. "Armando, Mister Ahmed has finished his coffee and I think he would like to go back to Albuquerque now."

Ahmed nodded and stood up from the table. "Thanks, Pastor, we'll be in touch. *Adios, aley-kom*, everyone."

As he watched the Muslim leave, Fr. Jake recalled a warning Armando had given him shortly after he arrived. *"They ain't gonna like you here."*

9 fr. jake's mass on sunday, august 22

In preparing for the 8:00 a.m. Mass in San Isidro Church, Fr. Jake ate an early breakfast then sat in his armchair to look over the readings for the Twenty-first Week of Ordinary Time. He intended to tell those who came to this Mass, and the ten o'clock service, about Carlotta having sold the store to a Muslim family. How might his congregation react to that news?

The First Reading was from the book of Isaiah. He read aloud, "Thus says the Lord of hosts, to Shebna, the master of the palace, 'I dismiss you from your office, I remove you from your post, and on the same day I call upon my servant Eliakim son of Hilkaiah. I invest him with your robe, I gird him with your sash, entrust him with your authority." *Hmm,* he thought, *that's rather appropriate, a change of responsibility, just as Mister Ahmed is taking over Carlotta's store. Probably not everyone here in Providencia, Catholic or not, will be pleased with the sale, but Jesus taught compassion and acceptance.* He turned the page. *How about the Second Reading? Any clues there?*

The reading was in Paul's letter to the Romans. "How rich are the depths of God, how deep his wisdom and knowledge and how impossible to penetrate his motives or understand his methods."

"Who could ever know the mind of the Lord?" Fr. Jake put down the book. *There could be a lesson there. Might God have been involved in a Muslim running the store to test, well maybe not test, but teach the value of tolerance to those living here? I'll ask Cynthia Plow to read a Koran and make a presentation about Islam at a meeting in her school. I do know that the religion honors Abraham and Jesus as prophets, yet not much more about it.* The priest glanced at his watch. "Seven-forty. Time get go over and get vested."

❧❧

The Vestry was not a separate room, only a small alcove at the back of the church. Armando and his *curandera* aunt sat, as usual, in three pews from the front. Fr. Jake had noted that most in the congregation stayed further back at most Catholic services. Cynthia passed out copies of missals with the day's readings that parishioners could follow. She had set out the wine and water cruets and a small water bowl in which the priest washed his hands. *Lavabo manus meus…* as the old Latin Mass had it. Now she came back to the priest. "All set Father, when you are," she told him.

"Thanks. Cynthia. You know, we have no deacon now, so I'd like to talk about getting you consecrated as one here at the church."

Taken somewhat aback, she flushed, and then stammered, "Me…Father? I…I'm a woman."

"True, but Saint Paul greets many women followers, and some were deacons. The word simply means ' helper' and you've been a great help here."

"Still—"

"We'll talk about it later, Cynthia, also about something I'd like you to do."

"Sure. What is it, Father?"

"Carlotta sold her store to a Muslim family named Ahmed," he told her. "The father, Bahir, will take over on September First. Hardly anyone living in Providencia knows about Islam, as the religion is called, and there might be some resentment at a non-Christian owning the store. Even acts of hostility."

"Then, Father, you must have an idea about how to inform the community."

"Correct," he said, "and that's where you come in. What I'd like you to do is make a presentation about the Muslim religion in a community meeting at the school. I'll get you a Koran so you can write up a summary of what Mohammed taught." Fr. Jake smiled. "Cynthia, you *are* a good school teacher, you know."

"Well sure, Father, I'd like to find out more about that religion myself. Now if you're ready, I'll ring the bell and you can proceed to the altar."

In his homily after the Gospel reading, Father Jake spoke about most in the congregation knowing about the sale of Carlotta's store to a man belonging to a religion other than Catholic or Protestant, but that he believed God had a purpose in doing so. He emphasized that Jesus and the Jewish religion had compassion, not only for the ill and lame, but also for the stranger among them. Even the outlawed Samaritans showed pity and aided an injured Jew.

On leaving after Mass, no one approached the priest to learn more about Ahmed or the sale, yet several in attendance expressed soft-spoken opinions among themselves, both pro and con.

10 cynthia plow and fr. jake visit dulci at the equus ranch

On Monday, August 23, Fr. Jake finished his usual breakfast of raisin bran and banana, then brought the cup of coffee to his armchair, sat down, and began his "Kitchen Mass" by opening his breviary to the First Reading for that day from the Book of Ruth.

"In the days of the Judges famine came to the land," he read aloud, "and a certain man from Bethlehem of Judah went with his wife and his two sons, to live in the country of Moab. Emil Lech, Naomi's husband, died, and she and her two sons were left. These married Moabite women were named Orpah and the other Ruth." Silently, he read on about how after ten years the sons and husband of Ruth also died. Ruth and her daughters-in-law returned to Moab because she heard the Lord had visited his people and given them food. "Not much there to influence my day," the priest muttered, but I'm afraid the Ahmed family could be moving into a new 'Moab.' Hopefully not. What about Responsorial Psalm 149? 'The Lamb has made us a kingdom of priests to serve our God. Allelulia!' That's much better, yet we also serve the faithful."

Each weekday Fr. Jake celebrated an 8:00 A. M. Mass, even thought it was sparsely attended, mostly retirees or the elderly. He would go fifteen minutes early to look over a Daily Missal and prepare a short homily based on the day's readings.

❧

After Mass Fr. Jake had returned to the rectory around 8:40, when a car horn blared outside. "That sounds like Cynthia's Hyundai Tucson. Wonder what she wants that she didn't mention at Mass yesterday?" He put his book down and went outside to meet her on the rectory porch.

"Good morning, Father," she called up to him from her open car door.

"Good morning, Cynthia. Is…is something wrong?"

"No, Father, nothing bad happened." She came up the stairs to shake his hand and say, "After Mass, during the day, I began to think that we should visit Dulcinea Trujillo…Dulci…and see how she's doing at the horse sanctuary. Would you have time to come with me today?"

"Yes, and it's an excellent idea, Cynthia. It will probably get quite warm today. Let me go inside to put on a short-sleeved shirt and my Roman collar. That will only take a minute"

"Sure, Father. Meet you in my car."

After Father Jake returned to the Hyundai and buckled himself in the passenger seat, Cynthia turned left on Highway 310, then right at Romero Loop to reach Rancho Tru-Cor property, now the horse sanctuary. Cynthia commented, "I remember being told that that Dulci is still quite distressed by the death of her father."

"Don Fernando wasn't a particularly good parent," Father Jake retorted. "He wanted to take his daughter to Mexico along with Millie, his mistress. Dulci didn't want to go."

Cynthia said, "I wasn't there yet, but wasn't her father pulling her by the hand to a waiting helicopter, when he saw you with two of his ranch hands. Fernando thought you'd try to stop him from leaving and fired a pistol to hit you and the ranch helpers."

"Fortunately he missed," Fr. Jake recalled.

Cynthia nodded. "I remember that you wanted to keep that helicopter from taking off and shouted for one of the ranch hands to throw barbed wire into the rotor. Bits of the wire flew forward and killed Fernando. Millie was injured and died later."

"Dulci saw all that horror and ran toward me." Fr. Jake shook his head, "She was trembling, repeating, 'I didn't want to leave' over and over. I told one of the ranch hands to take her back to the house, then called Sonia Mora on my cell."

"Father, a lot of us heard that helicopter land and drove out to see what was happening."

"Yes, Cynthia, that's when I saw your SUV, and asked you to go stay with Dulci."

"She was traumatized, of course, but still able to tell me what happened." Cynthia paused a moment, then continued, "Later on, Father, didn't you think it sort of 'miraculous' when those men from EQUUS showed up at her father's ranch property and offered to lease it as a horse sanctuary, with Dulci as the manager?"

"Miracles happen, Cynthia, and the men did have the names of angels didn't they? Gabriel and Rafael."

"Okay, Father. That was in July, let's go see how Dulci is doing now."

At the ranch entrance, the Rancho Tru-Cor sign had been replaced by one reading EQUUS Equine United Sanctuaries.

Cynthia spotted the Dulci at the far end of the field. "There she is, Father, evidently training an Arabian stallion. Miriam isn't with her."

Fr. Jake said, "I recall that Miriam was a mentor originally assigned to help Dulci adjust to being here."

"That's right. The sound of Cynthia's car pulling up had alerted the girl. She looked in that direction, waved, tethered the stallion, then walked toward her visitors. Dulci looked to be in good health: her blonde hair was pulled neatly back into a thick braid and her face was tanned. She wore jeans and a jacket with the Equus log sewn on the upper pocket.

Dulci greeted them, shaking hand with each. "Father, Cynthia. How nice to see both of you."

Cynthia asked, "We're not disturbing you are we? You looked quite busy up there."

Dulci explained, "I'm training a stallion for an upcoming American Quarter Horse Association Competition."

"Miriam doesn't help you any longer?"

"No she left. I'm pretty much on my own now."

That means Dulci is better, Fr. Jake thought and smiled. "That's great news to hear."

"Father, I got involved with AQHA, the association I mentioned. They sponsor a lot of competitions and give out prizes."

"So you're financially secure?" Cynthia want to know.

"I get paid by Equus, also they bought my father's ranch for the sanctuary and the balance of that money is in a trust fund until I'm twenty-one."

Fr. Jake suggested, "There could be another source of income for you. On this side of the river you're close to the Rio Grande Bosque. There are hiking trails, and you might get three or four mares and rent them out to people who like horseback riding. Advertise it in the newspaper."

"Hey, Father, what a great idea!" Dulci told the priest.

"I think so, too," Cynthia agreed. "Now maybe I'd better get Father back to the rectory. I interrupted what he was doing." She gave the girl a hug. "Bye for now, Dulci, I'll visit again."

Fr. Jake placed a hand on her head. "God Bless."

11 a stranger comes to fort liberty

Fort Liberty was a Survivalist compound surrounded by a razor wire fence and high boxwood hedge, with an earthen berm ten feet inside that concealed the fort's five buildings. An emergency exit was a narrow opening cut in the hedge on the south side. The main entrance was barred by an iron gate with a young guard in a camouflage uniform on duty, now sitting on a bench, in the shade of a maple tree, reading a comic book.

Milton Pointer, a man about 30 years old, stocky, with reddish hair, called out to him, "Hey, soldier! I need to come in and talk with Colonel Billy Ray Scurry."

The guard lowered the book but did not get up to ask, "What was your business with him? He got shot in the head an' killed last June."

"What, killed? Who…who are you?"

"Jon, his oldest son. I'm twenty-one. Be twenty-two in October. What's it to ya?"

"No offense, Jon, I'm truly sorry to hear of the Colonel's death. Like he was, I'm a Survivalist. That means against the government and for White racial purity. I've come to see what we can do about an Arab, a Muslim, who just bought Carlotta's grocery store."

"Okay, that does sound kinda serious."

"May I come in and talk to you about it?"

"Sure…." Jon got up to unlatch the gate and swing it open. Without closing it again, he started up a path with his unannounced visitor. "What did y' say your name was?"

"Milton Pointer."

"Okay."

Jon wore a faded Army camouflage uniform and floppy fatigue hat that had belonged to his father. He was tall, had blond hair, and was handsome in an unkempt way—camp discipline had lessened with Scurry's death.

Jon told his visitor, "Let's go to a bench at the shady side of our Command Post building."

"Lead the way, son."

After sitting down, Pointer extended a hand. "Sad about your father, Jon, and yet I'm glad to meet you as you'll surely carry on your father's work."

He returned a limp handshake; his father had warned that unexpected guys like this could be FBI agents snooping around for signs of drugs. Suspicious, he asked, "How d' you find out about this here compound?"

"I read a recent article about you and Fort Liberty in the *Socorro News Gazette*."

"You from Socorro?"

"No."

"Then why come here?"

"Jon, your father was a Colonel in the Gulf War. As I just told you, I'm a survivalist like he was, perhaps even more radical. My associates and I have been called white radical and neo-Nazi, yet the Germans lost World War Two and aren't a super race. Americans are or would be, except that this country is going to the dogs politically."

"What do y' mean by that?"

"Jon, we have a president, Barack Obama, born in Hawaii and not even an American citizen. A woman, Hilary Clinton, is Secretary of State. Another, Kagan, is on the Supreme Court. I've nothing against women, but do believe they shouldn't be given too much power. Do you have any such women at Fort Liberty?"

"Well, no," he admitted. "They mostly do the cookin' here."

"That's good," Pointer said, then asked, "Of what ethnicity are you, Jon?"

"Ethnicity?"

"What country in Europe did your father identify with?"

"He said we was Irish and damned proud of it."

"Well there you go," he went on. "You must know about Irish nationalists fomenting the Easter uprising against British rule in April,1917. The Irish republic was established."

"I did hear my daddy talk of it."

"That's what we want here, a change of government."

"Isn't that treason?" Alarmed now, Jon abruptly stood up. "Why did y'all come here?"

"Your grocery store and gas station here in Providencia has been bought by an Arab Muslim, a member of a non-white, non-Christian religion named Islam."

"And what do y' think my daddy woulda done about that?"

"You have gasoline here, don't you?"

"'Course, we got us a Hummer, other cars, too."

Pointer paused for a moment, before adding, "Jon Scurry, you're in charge now. What do *you* think your father would have done?" When the youth looked away and failed to reply, Pointer continued, "By the way, a priest serving at the church here had something to do with your father's murder. He shouldn't get away with it, should he?"

Jon stood up and extended a hand. "I got work t' do. Nice meetin' ya."

12 the trial of duane fortgang

Early on August 22, Fr. Jake's phone had rung as he was shaving before celebrating Mass. He wiped cream off half his face and answered, "Father. Jakubowski, Saint Isidro rectory. How may I help you?"

"Father this is Sonia Mora. I just received word that Duane Fortgang's trial will be on Tuesday, August 24, at one o'clock. The prosecutor wants us there as material witnesses."

"Aren't the charges cut and dry? We caught him in his van returning from a drug supplier in Mexico, where he obtains the cocaine he hides in his *santo* statues and sells."

"Sure, we'll testify to that, Father Jake, yet do you recall that he tried to confess to killing three other people? My uncle, Aimée Parker and Raylene? That would be very difficult to prove, but cocaine distribution and money laundering should put him behind bars for a good stretch of time."

"Deservedly so."

"Right, Father, so I'll come pick you up at Ten. On our way to Socorro we can discuss the case and our involvement in it. Maybe find out a bit more about you I'd like to know."

"I'll be ready.

"Fine. Good bye, Father Jake."

"Bye, Sonia."

The priest went back to finish shaving, but paused first to look in the mirror. "Seventy years old," he muttered. "White hair, healthy, and joking that 'seventy is the new fifty'. I better finish shaving, then brew some coffee and start preparing a homily for Sunday's Mass about the sale of Carlotta's store to a Muslim, Some villagers might not know about that. I wonder what their response will be?"

❧

Fr. Jake waited, sitting on a chair in the shade of the rectory's covered porch when the detective arrived in her red Plymouth Neon. The mud was gone; she had had the car cleaned at a car wash. Sonia wore her detective uniform—black slacks, shoes and jacket with her hair tucked under a Baker hat. The priest wore his Roman collar, a blue short-sleeved shirt, and dark slacks.

Sonia reached over to open the passenger door. "Buckle up, Father, Socorro is about a 45-minute drive."

"Sonia, that's plenty of time to find more about me than you probably want to know."

"I know you came here from Michigan. Were you born there?"

"No, in Krakow, Poland."

"Poland?"

The detective turned her car onto Highway 310 from the rectory driveway and headed south. Four miles along, a right turn led onto a bridge at Highway 60 that crossed the Rio Grande to reached Interstate 25. Socorro was some 25 miles distant from there.

On the bridge she continued, "I started to say that Poland is a long way from Michigan. I recall that you told me you were pastor of a parish there. So how did that happen?"

"After World War Two, in Poland two pre-war universities reopened, as well as Krakow seminary. Remember Communists were in power. At the seminary I met a priest named Karl Wojtyla who formed a sort of resistance group to keep the Catholic Church alive. I heard about it and joined at age Fifteen. Wojtyla eventually was appointed Auxiliary Bishop of Krakow and sponsored me to study at the Polish Orchard Lake Schools Seminary in Michigan."

"So that's how you got there."

"Yes, I was ordained in 1966, but, Sonia, shouldn't we be talking about Fortgang's trial? I don't know that much about how the legal system works."

"Father, he'll be assigned a defense attorney, yet he's a lawyer and may want to defend himself. The Courtroom isn't very large as it shares a space in the Municipal Building with the police and sheriff departments."

"Tell me a bit more about Socorro," Fr. Jake asked. "I think the word is Spanish for help or aid."

"Bravo, it does! Local history goes back to the late sixteenth century. Today, the New Mexico School of Mining and Technology is here. Also a mission church you'd appreciate, Father, San Miguel…." Sonia glanced at her watch. "It's only 11:33. No telling how long the trial might last so let's grab a light lunch. The Manzanares Coffee House has sandwiches and salads. It's near my apartment."

He nodded. "Sounds good to me."

Sonia turned right off I-25 and drove toward the small restaurant. A lunch crowd had not yet arrived to fill the place. They placed their orders, brought the food to a table near a window, and sat down.

Fr. Jake looked out the window. Socorro seems like a nice place to live, the little I've seen of it."

Sonia laughed. "Frommer's guide calls it a 'quiet pleasant town'."

Both had ordered focaccia bread sandwiches, a salad, and iced tea.

"Interestingly shaped bread, Sonia," Fr. Jake commented.

"I didn't know about it and asked. It's made of wheat flattened and oven-baked, a bit like pizza."

Each ate in silence. When Fr. Jake finished first, Sonia asked him, "Dessert? They have gelato."

"Thanks, I'll skip it"

"Same here."

Sonia drove back toward the County Courthouse. It was close to 12:25 when she pulled the Neon into the police parking lot. Inside the building, the two entered the courtroom. No one had yet come in.

"Father, the jury box is on the left, and so is the witness chair," Sonia pointed out. "I understand there will be six jurors. The table on the left is for the plaintiff and prosecuting attorney. On the right will be the defendant and his attorney, which might be Fortgang. The trial is about drug running, thus a criminal charge. She nodded toward three rows of seats ahead of them. "Let's go sit in the gallery until they call us."

Shortly after, when the trial attorneys and a prison guard escorting Fortgang entered the courtroom. Fortgang glanced at the priest and detective but did not acknowledge them.

"I recognize him," Fr. Jake whispered to Sonia. "Fiftish, balding, wearing glasses. He does look more pale and thinner."

"Prison and prison food, Father," Sonia quipped without smiling.

"He was from Amarillo, spoke with a Texas drawl. Quite arrogant. When we first met at San Isidro, he introduced himself as D. Duane Fortgang and told me to call him simply G.D." Fr. Jake noted, "Looks like's he's wearing a business suit."

Sonia explained, "We have a half dozen detention cells, Father. Since the trial is being held so soon after Fortgang's arrest, he was held there, along with a few belongings that included the suit. Let's see what happens."

At precisely 1:00 p.m. a call of "All Rise" was heard, as presiding Judge Karl Holloway came out of chambers and seated himself. Once there, everyone sat again. He banged his gavel, then announced, "The case is about the defendant, Duane Fortgang, obtaining cocaine in Mexico and bringing it to sell in New Mexico. How do you plead Mister Fortgang, guilty or not guilty?"

He replied, "I plead no contest Your Honor."

"No contest? Approach the bench."

Judge Holloway asked, "Mister Fortgang, are you aware that means you do not accept or deny the charge against you?"

"Your Honor, I'm a lawyer and know legal procedures."

"Very well." Holloway looked toward the jurors. "You are dismissed, thank you for your service. Mister Fortgang, you and the prosecuting and defending attorneys must meet with me in my chambers."

Fr. Jake looked at Sonia and asked, "No contest? What just happened?"

"Fortgang is shrewd," she told him. He knew he would be convicted and get a heavy sentence. Now, everyone the judge named will discuss the case. Fortgang won't say a thing but his court-appointed defense attorney will plea bargain for a lighter sentence. He'll still spend considerable time behind bars." She stood up. "Let's go, Father. I'll drive you back."

❧❧

As they drove north on I-25, both Sonia and Fr. Jake remained quiet, thinking about what had happened at the trial. Then Fr. Jake began to think of possible issues concerning another important matter in Providencia.

"Sonia," he said, "aside from Fortgang's trial, I've been wondering how Mister Ahmed, the Muslim who will take over Carlotta's store is doing. He and his family bought a house in Upland Estates and live there now."

Sonia nodded. "I heard about that, so let me know how it goes. Deadly violence against him could be planned by someone, even a group that resents the sale."

Fr. Jake sighed. "I sincerely hope not, Sonia."

13 pointer returns to fort liberty

At the Bellemonte Motel, where was he was staying, Milton Pointer waited in vain to hear a radio report, or read in the *Valencia County Herald*, about the torching of the store at Providencia that had been bought by its Muslim owner. Livid at the failure of Jon, eldest son of the deceased Billy Ray Scurry, to burn the store, on August 24 he had contacted an anti-Muslim colleague, William Bearce. He arrived at the motel in the late afternoon driving a Herzt-rented Ford car and wearing a short sleeved Tee shirt because of the heat. As his friend locked the car, Pointer noted a black tattoo around his neck and a star above one eye.

Pointer carried Bearce's small suitcase into a room he had rented next to his and thanked him. "I appreciate you coming here to help, Bill."

"No problem, Milt," he replied, "but you said that store was in Providencia. Belen is seven or eight miles away."

"I stayed here so not to be connected with the fire. Turns out Colonel Scurry was killed in June and now Jon, his son, runs the compound. The bastard hasn't done a damned thing so far. Look Bill, freshen up a bit and we'll talk over dinner. I have a plan. Did you bring your .38 Colt?"

"In a shoulder holster."

"Good. Keep it handy."

❧❧

The next morning, as Pointer directed him,. Bearce drove up the road to an iron gate at Fort Liberty's main entrance. The gate was ajar. A guard Pointer didn't recognize slouched, dozing on the bench where he had first seen Jon. Pointer said, "Bill, I'll go see if that's another of Scurry's sons." He got out of the car to pull the gate all the way open, and then went and shook the guard awake.

"Who the hell are you?" Pointer demanded.

Slowly rubbing sleep out of his eyes, the youth mumbled, "My name's Luke, Jon's younger brother."

"Where is Jon now?"

"In the command post."

"Fine...." Pointer walked back to the Ford's open driver's window. "Bill, the kid doesn't seem too bright. That's the Hummer up ahead I told you about. Now to get the keys to it."

He went back to Luke and said, "Son, I came to see Jon, but I'd love to take that Hummer for a short drive first. Like just a bit up the road and back."

"Sure go ahead. Key's in the ignition."

What luck! As planned, Pointer signaled for his accomplice to back out and drive slowly down to the store. He would take the Hummer and crash it into the gasoline pumps, then jump out.

Waiting for him to hurry back into the Ford, Bearce would throw a Molotov cocktail that would explode the gushing fuel, while they escaped in the Ford.

"Thanks, son, this'll only take a minute or two."

When Jon heard the Hummer start up, he came running out of the command post, saw Pointer in the driver's seat, and guessed correctly what he might do. "Son of a Bitch! Griego better be on duty down there and carryin' his belt phone!" He ran back to dial the sheriff.

Deputy Sheriff Hilario Griego had been assigned to park his patrol car nearby and prevent anyone from setting fire to the store.

When his belt phone rang, he answered, "Deputy Sheriff Griego."

"Deputy, this is Jon Scurry at the fort. A guy stole my Hummer and I think he's gonna crash it into the two gas pumps. Blow up the fucking place."

"Okay, I'm on it." Griego unholstered his service revolver and looked around. "Nothing, no one's even near here," he mumbled, squinting in the direction of the gravel road to the fort. In a few moments he saw a black Ford come down, cross the highway, and park a short distance away. "Just a guy shopping for groceries," he guessed.

A scant moment later he saw the Hummer speeding his way, heading straight for the gasoline pumps. "Holy shit!" Griego raised his gun with both hands, aimed carefully at the driver, then pulled the trigger. The bullet passed through the windshield and hit Pointer in the forehead. Driverless, the Hummer careened to the right, crossed the highway, and crashed into the Ford. Bearce, waiting to escape with Pointer, had not left his car and was slightly injured, thrown against the windshield in front.

Carlotta and a customer heard the noise and came out of the store to see what was happening.

Griego phoned for EMT Medics to arrive. The person driving the Hummer was DOA, so he went to see if he could help the man in the Ford. The driver's side window was open. Even with the airbag deployed, he was bleeding from a gash on his cheek. Deputy Griego jerked open the damaged side door and asked, "Sir, are you all right?"

Head slumped back, Bearce mumbled, "I told Milt this was a stupid idea."

"What, you're somehow involved in this incident?" Griego asked. "Uh, oh, what's that on your passenger seat? Seems like a bottle of gasoline, stoppered by a rag. He looked back at Bearce. "Sir, put your hands on the window sill, I'll have to handcuff you. Anything you say may be held against you in a court of law."

A distant siren indicted that an ambulance with emergency medical help was on its way.

14 an imam comes to providencia

News of an attempt to destroy the store appeared as a headline in the morning edition of the *Valencia County Herald*. Carlotta had called the editor of the newspaper, whom she knew from buying ads for her store in the past. Journalists from other newspapers read about the incident and now came to hear about what had happened from the store owner.

Ahmed had called his father, the Imam of the Mosque in Albuquerque, to tell him of the failed attempt. He told his son he would drive down. He also phoned Fr. Jake to tell him the news, who said he would stop by after his eight o'clock Mass.

⁖

Shortly after the store opened, Ahmed and Carlotta were outside, sweeping debris from the parking area when a dozen White-Supremacists, who read the paper and knew Pointer, arrived in in a van to picket the store and harass its Muslim owner. Most wore Army camouflage fatigues and helmet liners.

The leader, who refused to give his name, helped his followers set up a table taken from the van, also three American flags with the star field replaced by a circle on which was centered the Nazi Schutzstaffel SS symbol and surrounded by the group's name, ARYANS FIRST. Signs with derogatory terms for Muslims— "Fig-Gobblers," "Muzzies," and "Jihadists" were laid on the table. Two followers holding AK-47 rifles stood guard at each end. Both wore black Tee shirts with "Come And Take It" printed next to an AK-47.

Carlotta warned, "Mister Ahmed, this looks like trouble. I'm going inside to call Deputy Sheriff Griego. I'll tell him to bring a backup."

While she was in the store phoning, three men in leather jackets rode up on motorcycles. All had holstered revolvers slightly visible at their waists.

One dismounted, took off his helmet, approached one of the guards, and said, "Hey, Bro, we heard y'all were here. Need help picketing this Jihadist joint?"

"Hell yes." He indicated the table next to him with his AK-47. "You guys grab a sign and start marching around the pumps."

"What's with the 'Aryans First' flags?"

The man laughed. "If you ain't heard of us, Bro, ya soon will."

The group had barely picketed twice around the gasoline pumps when flashing red lights of the two Sheriff's patrol cars appeared, speeding their way on Highway 10. Both stopped, blocking the van and motorcycles to prevent any attempt of an escape.

Deputy Sheriff Hilario Griego stepped out of his patrol car, while the other Deputy stood next to his and watched, hand ready on his holstered service revolver.

Griego shouted, "Put your weapons down," then told the man nearest him, "Sir, we've just received a call about a disturbance of the peace. Who's in charge here?"

The leader of Aryans First came forward. "I am, exercising my constitutional right to peaceful assembly."

"That your van over there?" the sheriff asked.

"It is."

"Sir, show me your van registration, driver's license, and insurance document."

The man reluctantly took out his wallet from a side pocket to find and then hand the sheriff what he had asked for.

Griego read the name on the license. "David Tripp?"

After he nodded, the sheriff said, "Seems like a lot of weapons for a peaceful assembly. Also the store owners who called us said you were harassing them by picketing the place with signs that had anti-Muslim slurs lettered on them. There's one of them on the ground." He indicated a bulge on Tripp's right side. "Sir, have you paid the One hundred dollar handgun fee and have a Certificate?"

Before Tripp could answer, the other Sheriff had gone over to question the three motorcyclists. Now he called over, "Griego, everyone here is carrying a concealed weapon."

"Ask for their Certificates, Griego said. "And what about those AK-47's? The Open Carry law allows them unless they frighten someone and I'd bet Carlotta is freaked out. We'll get some crime tape up around the store, but call for a police van first. Everyone we've questioned, stay where you are, or risk being an unlawful fugitive and tracked down."

Just then, Fr. Jake walked up, and then stopped to look at what had happened.

"Stay back, Father," Griego called to him. "This is a crime scene."

Moments later the Imam's car, a GMC Acadia SUV, with **Islamic Center of Albuquerque** stenciled on the side, stopped a short distance away. Ahmed saw it and hurried over to greet his father. Abdul, the driver, opened the passenger door for Imam Bahir Ahmed Muhammad.

After the Imam stepped out to survey the damage, Fr. Jake saw Ahmed beckon him over to be introduced. The Imam was of middle height, bearded, and dressed in an ankle-length robe. A tight-fitting soft turban covered his hair.

When Fr. Jake came over, Ahmed said, "*Ab*…Father…this is Pastor Jaku, who supported me as the new owner of the store."

The Imam extended a hand. "I am grateful, Pastor," he told him in unaccented English. "As I see here it seems not everyone was happy at the sale to a Muslim."

Fr. Jake shook his head in dismay. "Unfortunately, Imam, we have a rise in hate and extremist groups lately, such as the Neo Nazis and White Supremacists."

The Imam shook his head at the thought of more possible violence.

Ahmed said to his father, "*Ab* you've not seen the house we bought and it's close by. Amina is there with the children. Let's drive up and see them before you go back to Albuquerque."

The Imam smiled. "Bahir, I was about to suggest doing exactly that. I would not want to miss seeing your wife and my grandchildren."

"Abdul can drive us up," Bahir said and turned to the priest. "Pastor Jaku, you come, too. Perhaps we can come up with ways to counter the extremist groups you mentioned."

After they were seated in the van, Bahir told Abdul, "Drive up the gravel road to the street that's paved, then turn right. Ours is the first house, number twenty. You can park in the driveway."

The house was a medium-size adobe-styled stucco compared to the larger homes further up where Duane Fortgang had lived. Ahmed's was a Territorial style with a porch on two sides.

About 1,800 square feet Fr. Jake thought to himself. *Probably three bedrooms and two baths, large enough for the Ahmed family and a mortgage they can afford. There must be another mortgage because they purchased Carlotta's store.*

The entrance door was painted blue, a color deemed to bring good luck in New Mexico. Amina had heard the van pull up and waited there with her two children on the front porch.

Abdul stayed in the van. The Imam was the first person out of the vehicle and greeted Amina in Arabic, "*Assalam'alaykom.* Peace be on you."

"*Alaykom assalaam,*" she replied, and smiling, added, *Ahlan wa sahlan.* Welcome, Father-in-Law."

The two children, Galeb and Dalia, had run back inside, frightened perhaps by the strange man in a long robe.

"Good morning, Father Jaku," Amina said, stepping aside. "Welcome, to our home. Come in."

"I'm pleased to meet the Imam and that your husband invited me," Fr. Jake told her. "Bahir and I may be able to figure out ways to frustrate those extremists picketing the store today."

"Allah willing," she commented softly.

The door opened up into a spacious living room. The kitchen and other rooms were to the right.

"I'll make tea," Amina said. "We have a few honey pastries left to eat."

The Imam asked, "Where are Galeb and Dalia?"

"They're bashful and probably hiding in their rooms. Both aren't used to seeing you in a robe like you have on, my Father-in-Law."

He laughed. "And I'll take off now that I'm not in public. Where may I do that?"

"In our bedroom. Come, I'll show you where it is."

A leather sofa faced a wall, with a coffee table in front. Bahir indicated them and said, "Pastor Jaku, please make yourself comfortable."

"Thanks," Fr. Jake replied. "I was admiring several pictures on your far wall."

"Mostly done in Arabic calligraphy."

"The largest is lettered in English," Fr. Jake noted, then read off, "'Dignity, Reverence. Serenity, High Aspiration.'"

"All attributed to the Quran, Pastor."

"Those also are Christian virtues—"

Bahir said, "Of course you know that we worship one God between us."

The Imam returned wearing a white shirt and dark trousers, but had left his turban on. "Dressed like this, now I shouldn't frighten my grandchildren. Bahir please go fetch them."

Fr. Jake said, "Imam, I was mentioning to your son that I like the art on that wall."

"Yes, and without human figures, although some medieval works show them…. Ah, here are my grandchildren."

Galeb and Dalia walked slowly into the living room urged in by their father. "That man is your grandfather," Bahir told them. "Go give him a hug."

The two children seemed reluctant to do so, yet obeyed their father.

The Imam gave each a light kiss on the cheek, and told them, "You are fine looking children. May you grow up in obedience to the teachings of the Quran and Allah."

A bit strong for children that young, Fr. Jake thought, then saw Amina come in carrying a tray with a tea pot, cups, napkins, and a plate of honey pastries. *I wonder if Muslims pray before eating?*

Amina laid the tray on the coffee table then poured out cups of tea. "Please help yourselves," she said, handing Fr. Jake a cup of tea. "Pastor Jaku."

"Thank you." After taking a sip and bite of pastry, Fr. Jake asked, "Imam, I know you were born in this country, but where were your grandparents from?"

"Like many immigrant Arabs, from Lebanon," he answered. "Times were perilous…civil war…unrest. They were merchants and, fortunately, had enough money to leave."

"Imam, you are the head of a Mosque in Albuquerque. About how many Muslims, would you say, live in New Mexico?" Fr. Jake asked.

"Perhaps three hundred. Most are businessmen or teachers, lawyers… professionals. None farm."

"And your son now owns a store here in Providencia." Fr. Jake turned to ask, "Bahir, will you still sell beer and wine? Those *santos* figures that tourists buy?"

Bahir smiled. "Pastor, didn't you hear my father say we were businessmen? Of course, although I am concerned about that armed opposition we saw today. Didn't you say you had a plan for dealing with that?"

"Yes, I financially support the Anti-Hate Watch Legal Center at Washington D.C.," he answered. "The Center keeps track of individuals or hate groups like Neo- Nazis that violate civil rights and file court injunctions that fines them thousands of dollars and a possible loss of their land."

"That is encouraging, Pastor," the Imam said. "At least something is being done."

"Yes…." Fr. Jake stood up. "I should be getting back to the rectory. Parishioners may want to find out more about what happened today."

Bahir joined him in standing up. "Abdul can take you back in the van. He's waiting outside and knows where your church is."

"Thank you." Fr. Jake went to shake hands with the Imam. "A pleasure speaking with you, sir, and knowing more about your background."

"Peace be on you, Pastor," he said, returning the handshake.

"Amina, your refreshments were delicious," Fr. Jake told her from the door.

She handed him a small bag. "Pastor these are a few honey pastries to eat with your coffee."

"*Gracias*, Amina. "Goodbye, children."

Bahir went to the van with Fr. Jake and spoke in Arabic about taking the Pastor back to his church.

The priest sat next to Abdul in the van's passenger seat, but the Muslim did not speak as they drove to San Isidro. Several people were still gathered in front of store, talking about what had happened that morning.

When the van reached San Isidro church, Fr. Jake noticed Cynthia's Tucson was in the parking lot, next to another car.

After Abdul stopped, Fr. Jake opened the door to step out, then turned to thank the driver. "*Gracias. Assalaam 'alaykom.* Peace be on you."

"*Alaykom assalaam*," he responded in Arabic, and then added, "Good bye," in English.

Cynthia had seen the van and the priest step out of it. "Over here, Father," she called to him. "I'm with Francisco."

He looks vaguely familiar, Fr. Jake thought as he walked closer. *I believe he's the person who leaves early, before the last Gospel.*

Cynthia introduced him. "Father, this is Francisco Oñate I just met him here and he wants to talk to you."

Oñate reached to shake the priest's hand. "A pleasure, Father, and I do apologize for leaving Mass early."

"Do you live in Providencia?"

"Not yet, but I'm hoping to do so."

"Father," Cynthia said, "I'm excited. You know how I'm an amateur archaeologist. Well, Francisco is a lawyer, but also a historian. He found out about our empty community center and has a great idea for using it."

"And I'm eager to hear what it is, and also more about Francisco," the priest said, and held up the bag Amina had given him. "It's too warm for coffee, but a glass of wine would go quite well these pastries. Let's walk back to the rectory and find out."

Cynthia gave Francisco her questioning "should we" look.

"Providencia is full of great ideas," he remarked, "and I'm going to like it here. Let's go!"

15 the community center becomes useful

When they returned to the rectory and went inside, Fr. Jake brought out his opened bottle of Côtes du Rhone, then took three wine glasses from a small walnut-stained cabinet above the sink and set them on the kitchen table. Cynthia and Francisco stood by and watched him.

"We probably should sit in here," Fr. Jake told them. "It's the coolest place in the rectory at this hour."

"Fine with me, Father," Cynthia agreed. "Francisco?"

"Ditto."

Fr. Jake said, "Sit down at the table and I'll pour the wine. Cynthia, open that bag of honey pastries that Amina gave me. I'll put them on napkins."

When she and Francisco were seated, the priest half-filled their glasses, set them in front of the two, then held up his glass. "What shall we toast?"

Francisco suggested, "How about to the success of the Community Center?"

"Bravo!" Fr. Jake exclaimed. "Hold up your glasses…together. To the success of the Community Center!"

After each took a sip, Father Jake sat down opposite the two. "Francisco, the stage is yours, as the saying goes. Tell us about your background, your family name of Oñate."

"Cynthia teaches about the Conquistador, Juan de Oñate, in her history class. Perhaps she should do the talking."

"Francisco—" Cynthia warned.

"All right. Tradition is that Juan was born around 1550, the son of well-off parents in Zaca-New Spain, what we call Mexico today. After he married a granddaughter of Hernando Cortés his future was pretty much secured. Juan's petition for authority to conquer, settle, and govern New Mexico was approved in 1595, but it took three years to find about four hundred families willing to join him." Francisco looked up. "Am I boring you Father?"

"Not at all," Fr. Jake replied, "but why did your parents name you after Saint Francis of Asissi, one of my favorite saints?"

"I'm not sure, but they dropped the 'de' from Oñate. Juan de Oñate wasn't exactly a role model for them."

"Please continue, Francisco. Where did the Conquistador lead his colonists?"

"They crossed the Rio Grande at El Paso, where de Oñate established a kind of base camp at a point where the river confluences with the Chama. It wasn't good farm country, so he sent outsearch parties to find a rumored treasure of Quivira, one that never existed. Food was getting scarce, and the remaining settlers grumbled about returning to Mexico but he refused, even executed a few. He ordered them to raid Indian pueblos for food, while he set out to search for the treasure." Francisco laughed. "The way I put it is the Indians told him, 'Oh yeah, we heard about that. It's just a bit further, so keep going.' That led him past Taos Pueblo and as far north as today's Kansas. At that point he finally realized he had been flummoxed and turned back—"

"Let's take a break here," Cynthia, suggested. "Father, some of your coffee might be in order, now and we won't be going to look over the community center until tomorrow."

"It's about time for lunch," Fr. Jake told her after glancing at his watch. "I could rustle up some frozen Lasagna from Carlotta's that I have, or we could go see if Mamacita's is open."

"Too much bother for you, Father," Francisco said. "If I'm moving here, I'll need to be familiar with a restaurant."

Cynthia said, "Leave your car here, Francisco, and I'll drive there. Let's go."

The restaurant was open but not heavily patronized because of the morning's trouble.

Julia was on duty and saw Fr. Jake come in with Cynthia and man she didn't know. The waitress directed them to a table and took out her order pad. "We have plenty of *Huevos Rancheros* today, Father. Can I bring an order for all of you?" she asked.

"Sure, Julia" Fr. Jake agreed, "but first let me introduce Mister Francisco Oñate. He'll be moving here from Belén and said he would need a good restaurant."

Francisco shook Julia's hand, adding, "Father recommended this as a great one."

"Thanks, sir," she responded, blushing slightly. "I…I'll bring the eggs. Coffee all around? Water?"

"Please, Julia," Father Jake told her, then asked, "Francisco have you had the egg style Julia mentioned?"

"Can't say I have, Father."

"Julia?"

She said, "Two eggs fried in bacon drippings and green chile stew poured over the eggs. Served with tortillas and fried potatoes."

"And enough food to skip dinner," Francisco jested.

"Glad you mentioned that," Fr. Jake told him. "Rather than drive back to Belén, you can stay in the rectory tonight. I don't have a spare bedroom, but the couch in the living room is sleep-able."

"Give me a call and I'll meet you both there," Cynthia said, nervously brushing back a cluster of auburn hair.

"I'll be sure to do that." Francesco smiled and Fr. Jake thought he caught his slight wink at Cynthia's agitation.

Julia brought the coffee and water, and smiled. "Eggs will be done in a minute."

Francisco took a sip of coffee, then put his cup down. "Look, what we were talking about at the rectory. I don't want to drive it into the ground, but sixty years before Juan de Oñate went out searching for the Quivira treasure, Vasquez de Coronado traveled the same route in looking for the Seven Cities of Gold…Eldorado…and also was told to go as far as Oñate did. There's even a Coronado State Park in Kansas. Seems my ancestor wasn't too bright—"

"Enjoy your meal," Julia interrupted, setting down the three platters of food. "More coffee?"

"Please."

Fr. Jake and the others crossed themselves to recite the Catholic prayer before meals in unison. "Bless us, Oh, Lord and these thy gifts, which we are about to receive from thy bounty, through Christ Our Lord. Amen."

Francisco tasted a forkful of his meal and nodded approval. "I like these rancher's eggs."

"Try a 'torcilla'," Cynthia quipped, then said, "I'm looking forward to seeing that community building tomorrow. Father, do you remember what it was like inside?"

"Let's see, I only went in once and got in because one of the double doors was open. The main multipurpose room was littered with all kinds of trash. Four large windows on either side were boarded up. There was a kitchen on the left, with restrooms and class or meeting rooms on one side of a hallway."

"Great!" Francisco exclaimed, "and just what we need for our purpose in making the Center useful to both children and adults. After school and summer activities for kids, perhaps a meal program for senior citizens."

"Ambitious," Fr. Jake said. "I'll bring a flashlight, but we should take the boards off one of the windows on both sides to see well."

"I have a hammer and prying bar I can bring," Cynthia added, then asked, "Father, aren't you celebrating Mass tomorrow morning?"

"Yes, at eight o'clock as usual. Francisco is staying with me overnight, so I'll bring him to Mass and we can go to the community center right afterwards."

They had finished eating when Julia came to ask if they wanted dessert. No one did, so she tore off a page from her order pad. Father reached back for his wallet, but Francisco had already picked up the bill.

"This is on me," he said, standing. "Least I can do in light of your hospitality."

"I'll leave Julia a tip," Fr. Jake said.

"I should go to my classroom," Cynthia remarked. "School starts soon and I still have lesson plans to work on."

"Francisco," Fr. Jake suggested, "how about taking a stroll along the highway to show you a bit more about Providencia, since you plan on moving here?"

"Great idea. See you tomorrow, Cynthia."

"You'll be walking past my school, Exceléncia Elementary," she told him. "The ruins of Civil War Fort Providence are behind the building, where I'd been excavating earlier this year."

"And that's what gave the village its name of Providencia."

"Right on, Francisco! See you *mañana*. So long, Father," Cynthia said.

"God Bless," he replied, touching her forehead.

Outside, Francisco looked around. "Which way should we go?"

"Let's walk south toward Cynthia's school."

They had gone a short distance in silence, when Francisco asked, "Father, Cynthia told me you came here from Michigan, yet were born in Poland. How is it that you were assigned to a parish in New Mexico, of all places?"

"It's still temporary. I do have a parish in Michigan, but was sent here to help an ill, dysfunctional priest at San Isidro, Father Jésus Mora."

"Were you able to help him?"

"Well…actually he was murdered."

"What?"

"Francisco, he was the uncle of a Socorro woman detective, Sonia Mora. In the six months I've been here, she and I have been involved in solving several crimes. I've gotten to know Sonia quite well and respect her work. Do you still want to move here despite all the 'crime'?"

"Absolutely."

"Good. You know, I've wondered about your Oñate surname," Fr. Jake told him. "Did it originate in Spain?"

"Catalonia," he explained. "In truth it's not that unusual a name. There are quite a number of people with the Oñate surname in South America, and even a few in Switzerland."

"Imagine that." Fr. Jake looked around. "Here we are at Cynthia's school. That small building up ahead is a Pentecostal church. Elder Jerimiah is the presbyter, and I recall he said that San Isidro was 'The House of Idolatry' because we have statutes inside, hand carved wooden *santos* really."

"Hold on, Father," Francisco said. "Don't the most radical evangelicals consider our Catholic Church to be the Devil's work?"

"I don't believe Jerimiah goes that far," Fr. Jake said. "He just objects to the *santos*, which really are a Hispanic Catholic tradition."

"And like Muslims, Pentecostals don't have them," Francisco said, then asked, "Father, are you ready to return to the rectory? We have a big day ahead us tomorrow."

"Sure, let's go back."

16 realizing the community center's problems

While Francisco still slept on the couch in the sitting room, tired out by the long previous day, Father Jake was up early to brew coffee and prepare two bran and banana breakfasts, and then read his Breviary for Thursday, August 26. He sat down at the kitchen table, to not disturb his guest, took a sip of coffee, and read quietly from Paul's first letter to the Thessalonians. "Brothers, your faith has been a great comfort to us in the middle of our own troubles and sorrows. Now we can breathe again as you are still holding firm in the Lord." *We certainly have had troubles here yesterday*, he thought. *Let's see how Paul resolved his problems.* "How can we thank God enough for you, for all the joy we feel before our God on your account? We are earnestly praying night and day to be able to see you face to face again and be able to —"

"Am I bothering you, Father?" Francisco asked. "I'm all dressed."

Fr. Jake looked up the see him in the doorway. "Not at all, come and have breakfast. I usually read my Breviary to see if the readings have any bearing on my day. Paul's letter to the Thessalonians seems to say so."

"In what way?"

"Sit down, please. We can start eating and I'll tell you." The priest put his Breviary down and stood up to fill his guest's coffee cup and set it next to him. "Francisco, your bowl has my standard bran and banana breakfast. I don't pray in the morning before eating."

"Okay. When in Rome…." he began.

"Do as the New Mexican's do," Fr. Jake finished the saying. Both laughed.

After eating a spoonful of cereal, Francisco asked, "What did Paul say?"

"Paul speaks of troubles and sorrows and I'm afraid that's what we'll encounter in trying to make the community center a place of happiness."

"Isn't our plan to make it a one of usefulness to the residents here?"

"Today's Responsorial Psalm today is, 'Fill us with your love, O Lord, and we will sing for joy'!"

"We'll be working at the Center out of love and, hopefully, not 'off-key', regarding what we do there."

"Aptly put, Francisco." Fr. Jake looked at his wrist watch. "When we're finished, I'll put our dishes in the sink and we'll walk over to the church for Mass. Cynthia will have the altar ready. She's a kind of 'altar girl.' A few parishes have them. I think she's going to ask you to be parish financial officer, that is, deposit Sunday envelope offerings in Western Bank at Belén."

"Won't be difficult," he said. "That's my bank too."

Inside San Isidro, the usual small number of elderly or retired Catholics were scattered among the pews; only three or four worshipers ever sat near the front. Francisco sat next to one of them. Cynthia had put the wine and water cruets and a chalice on a small side table, and lighted two candles. She stood in the doorway of the vestry, dressed in blue denim work overalls. When she saw Fr. Jake and Francisco come in, she gave them a half-smile and quick wave of her hand.

Fr. Jake vested in a green Chasuble, came out to kneel on a stair in front of the altar, to make the sign of the cross and begin Mass.

"In the name of the Father, and of the Son, and of the Holy Spirit."

❧❧

At the end of Mass, Cynthia and Francisco waited at the front door of the church for Father Jake to take off his vestments.

"This is the big day we've been waiting for to work on the community center," she told Francisco. "Are you ready?"

He joked, "I didn't bring any tools, just my brawn."

"Guess that will have to do…. Here comes Father. Let's get in my car and drive over."

While Cynthia waited to cross Highway 10, Fr. Jake told her. "Stop in front of Armando's before we get to the building. I want to introduce Francisco to him."

"Good idea, just in case he has car trouble."

At his car repair shop, Armando was changing a tire on an automobile. When he saw Cynthia's Tucson, and her passengers, he came over to ask, "What kinda car trouble ya got, Cindy?" he asked.

"With luck, none," she replied, "but I want to introduce you to Francisco Oñate. He's moving here in a little while."

After Francisco shook hands with him, Armando asked, "What kinda car ya got?

"2008 Buick."

"Spiffy car—"

"Armando," Fr. Jake interrupted, "We're here to work on making the community center building useable. Can you tell us something about it?"

"Not much. 'Bout a year or so ago, a Valencia County Commissioner… forget his name…he wanted to be re-elected and thought building the place would do the trick. Heck, we just didn't know what to do with it, so it just it just sat there."

Fr. Jake said, "I've been inside and if it was only built a year ago it's in pretty good shape. Cynthia, drive up closer and we'll go in. I brought along a flashlight."

A large weathered sign above the twin entrance doors had been lettered PROVIDENCIA COMMUNITY CENTER. One blue door was open.

"Cynthia…Francisco…after you," Fr. Jake said as he pulled open the other door to admit more light.

Once inside, Francisco smacked his forehead and exclaimed, "What an unbelievable mess!"

Cynthia said, "Sure, it will take a lot of money and at least a year to finish, but it's what we agreed to help do."

"I'll be of any use I can now," Fr. Jake offered, "but won't be here to see it."

Alarmed, Cynthia asked, "What do you mean, Father?"

"Remember, this was a temporary assignment to help Father Mora," he told her. "I still have a parish in Michigan, and any day now I may be recalled to serve that one."

"Then who will be the priest at San Isidro?"

"Archbishop Benisek will appoint someone. Cynthia, we came here to discuss ways to open this building, so let's start."

Francisco said, "We'll have to present our case to the State Legislature in order to obtain funding. As an attorney, I can do that, but they won't meet again until January 2011."

Cynthia objected, "The Legislators won't come out here to look at the building and see if it's worth the money. Most will never even have heard of Providencia."

"You'll have at least one legislator there," Francisco told her, then suggested, "You could have your class make cardboard models of the Center to show what it will be like."

Fr. Jake added, "They'll want a budget. The largest cost would be a Director's salary, and that of a teaching staff of at least two who would schedule activities. Of course, a janitor. At your presentation, point out that local business sponsors could involve VISTA…Volunteers in Service to America…at no cost. Most approved applicants are retired teachers and can be here for three years, a good start. One setback is that they may not approve of funding the first time we apply. Make darn sure you have the best presentation."

Francisco brushed a hand through his hair. "We can't do much more today, and I have to get back to Belén. My apartment lease is up on the 31st so I'll have to move."

Cynthia commented, "Providencia doesn't have apartments."

"Exactly, so I'd like to buy a house in that Upland Heights subdivision. Nothing too large… two bedrooms or something like that." Francisco turned to the priest. "Father, I won't impose on you any longer, so I'll drive back to Belén now and not stay overnight again."

"No imposition at all," Fr. Jake said, "and a pleasure to have met you. As to the Center, I'll get Armando to help taking down the boards over the two windows, and have him put a lock on the doors so the inside won't be trashed."

Francisco said, "That would be of great help. Cynthia…'Cindy'… didn't Armando call you that?" Could you drive us back to my car in the church parking lot and I'll get on the road."

"Sure thing. 'Cindy' is a nickname Armando gave me, like some people call him 'Mando.'"

"No big deal."

When they stepped outside an older man stood looking at the building, saw the group come out, and asked, "Are you planning to open the Center? I hope so."

"Sorry, who are you?" Fr. Jake asked him.

"Fred Henderson, Reverend. I'm a World War Two veteran."

"Where did you serve?"

"I was a Sergeant in the 101st Airborne, one of the guys who parachuted into Normandy on June 6, 1944. I just turned 85."

Fr. Jake reached to shake his hand, and then introduced the others. "This is Cynthia Plow and Francisco Oñate. They'll help in opening up the Center."

"A pleasure, Sergeant," they both told him, shaking hands.

"Do you live in Providencia?" Fr. Jake asked.

"I was born in Albuquerque, Reverend, stayed in the Army, and then retired down here for some peace and quiet. After what I saw of war in France and Germany, afraid I'm not much of a church-goer."

Blaming God Fr. Jake thought, then said, "Sergeant Henderson, the Center probably won't be open for at least a year, but you'll be welcome to take advantage of what it has of interest to you."

"Appreciate it." he replied. "Have a nice day."

"You too. Goodbye, sir, and spread the word about the Center to your buddies," Francisco told him.

"You bet. So long."

Cynthia said, "Get in my car and I'll drive back to the church parking lot."

At the Buick, Cynthia watched while Francisco unlocked the driver's side door and stood outside. Fr. Jake brought out his small overnight case from the rectory.

"Don't forget this."

"Thanks, Father, I'll toss that on the back seat." He shook the priest's hand. "Again, thanks for your hospitality."

"My pleasure in meeting you," he replied.

Francisco turned to Cynthia and gave her a hug. "I'll stay in touch."

"Please call me every once in a while."

He nodded and slid into the driver's seat and turned on the engine. She closed the door, warning, "Drive carefully."

Francisco put two fingers to his lips in a sign of affection. "Will do." He released the parking brake, gunned the Buick onto Highway 10, and drove to the right.

Both watched him leave, then Fr. Jake turned to Cynthia and smiled. "Did I detect a bit of romance in the air?"

"I like him, Father, but let's leave it there for now. I've got lesson plans to work out."

"Cynthia, he seems attracted to you," Fr. Jake insisted, "and you both have much in common."

"I haven't known Francisco that long, Father," she told him. "We've just met at a history conference at the Belén library."

"Okay, no rush," Fr. Jake said. "Go do your lesson plans, and God bless."

17 jon scurry comes to see father jake on august 27

At about 10: 45 in the next morning, wearing a denim jacket that barely concealed a .45 caliber pistol holstered around his waist, Jon Scurry had parked his pickup truck on the street and now banged on the locked door of San Isidro church with a fist. Frustrated, he called to a man passing by.

"Hey, how come the *Padre* ain't openin' this door? Can't he hear me?"

"Father Jake doesn't live in the church. He'd be in his rectory."

"Wrecketry? What's that?"

The man pointed beyond the church. "See that adobe house with a metal roof. Just drive up the gravel road, Father's probably in at this hour."

"Okay."

At the rectory, the priest had eaten breakfast and now sat in his armchair to read the passage in his Breviary for Friday, August 27.

"Paul's letter to the Thessalonians," he read aloud. "'Brothers, we appeal to you in the Lord Jesus to make more and more progress in the kind of life that you are meant to live, the life that God wants, as you have learnt from us and that you are already living. You have not forgotten the instructions we gave you on the authority of the Lord Jesus. What God wants is for you to be holy. He wants you to keep away from fornication and for each of you to know how to use the body that belongs to him in a way that is holy and honorable, not giving way to selfish lust like the pagans who do not know God. He wants nobody at all to sin by talking advantage of a brother in these matters. The Lord always punishes sins of that sort as we told you before and assured you. We have been called—'"

Rough knocking on his front door interrupted Fr. Jake. The priest laid down his Breviary and stood up to open the door.

A young man waited there. He looked upset, shifting his weight from foot to foot, glancing from side to side and back over his shoulder.

"May I help you?" Fr. Jake asked.

"*Padre*, ya probably don't remember me but I met ya once last June. I'm Jon Scurry, eldest son of Billy Ray Scurry up at Fort Liberty. I need t' talk."

"Of course, come in. Can I get you coffee?"

"I'm good."

"Then let's sit down over here in my small living room." Once seated, Fr. Jake asked, "What's with the gun?"

"Normal thing t' wear one up at the Fort. By the way, my name's spelled J-o-n."

"Jon, what do you want to discuss with me?"

"I guess you might of heard what happened at the store yesterday? Them gas pumps?"

"I did. Sheriff Griego briefed me. I was happy I didn't have to administer the last rites to anyone."

"Whatever, but that was my Hummer and this guy…I forget his name… tried to use it to blow up the place."

"Because Carlotta sold the store to a Muslim. Jon, it was an act of retribution…intolerance."

"That got me to thinkin' half the night. I got three brothers and dad didn't tell us much of what he believed…what was going on. He just made us work, keep the place clean, practice shooting, stuff like that."

"Go on."

"Bein' a'sovereign citizens' for one. Common law another, like you just could go into an empty house, put it up a sign, an' take it over, Some shit…sorry *padre*…somethin' like setting up a Sovereign Republic outside the USA. That's treason. By the way, that guy what stole my Hummer said you killed my dad. Why?"

"Jon, I didn't kill him. During a drug raid, your father had a pistol pointed at me. It was a deacon at my church who shot him to save me."

"You ain't lyin to me?"

"I'm not—"

At that point the telephone rang.

"Excuse me a moment, Jon." The priest got up and answered, "Father Jakubowski, San Isidro, how may—"

Amina Ahmed's frantic voice interrupted him. "Pastor, our daughter Dalia has been kidnapped."

"What Amina?"

"She and Galeb were at the school, helping that teacher when Dalia got tired and started to walk home. The first we knew of it I was when I got a phone call from one of those white suprematists that picketed the store. He said he had our daughter and gave Bahir an hour to get $10,000 from our bank in Belén."

"Ransom money," Fr. Jake speculated.

"Yes. He warned us not to call the police or sheriff."

"Where are you to give him the money?"

Amina said, "Pastor, he doesn't trust us and wants you to do that. After I hang up you'll get a call from him. I…I'm going to do that now."

Fr. Jake was frowning and white faced with shock when he put down the receiver and looked over at Jon.

"Bad news, *padre?*" he asked. "You don't look too good."

"More poor news to come—"

The phone rang again.

"I better go now," Jon said. "You're pretty busy."

"No, wait." Father Jake pulled him back by the arm, and then picked up the phone. "San Isidro. How may I help you?"

"You already damn well know that, Parson. That Muslum woman called you."

"Yes, what's your name?"

"That's not important."

Fr. Jake tried to keep his voice calm. "I'll have to know where you're located to bring you the ransom money."

"Right, but you have ta swear on your oath as a Parson not to tell anyone."

That's only in confession but he doesn't know that. Fr. Jake pushed a notepad and pencil toward Jon and mimicked a writing motion. "Go ahead, I swear to keep silent."

"Okay, you know that funny lookin' buildin' by the river that isn't a church but looks like one."

"The Morada," he said then pointed at Jon to write down the name.

"What time?"

"You got the money?"

"The girl's mother does. I can go get it."

"Okay, but you come alone, damn it. Drive your car and park fifty feet from my van. How long will it take you to get here?"

"Half hour…forty-five minutes. Don't harm the little girl—"

"He hung up, Jon. I'll need your help with this," Fr. Jake said. *And your gun*, he thought in desperation.

"Sure, *padre*. How can I do that?"

"A white supremacist that picketed the store the day after the gasoline pumps were attacked kidnapped the eight-year-old daughter of the Muslim family and wants ransom money. He didn't tell me his name, but I don't believe he'll free the girl. He might kill her and me too. He'll need to get away in a hurry."

"Son of bitch!" Jon exclaimed. "What can we do about it?"

"Besides that gun you wear, do you own a rifle?" Fr. Jake asked.

"You bet. I got me an M-I Garand mounted in the back window of my TITAN Pickup outside."

"World War Two. Jon, take it down and put it in my Nissan. We'll leave right away."

"*Padre*, do you have the ransom money?"

"No, but I'll bring along a suitcase of mine to make the kidnapper believe I have. Let's go."

After Jon put the rifle in his car and got in, Fr. Jake drove the Nissan and turned left on Highway 10 to reach Romero Loop.

"Have you seen the Morada, Jon?" the priest asked. "It isn't used much, just during Lent."

"Lent? What's that?"

"Never mind. It's reached by a dirt road and there's a lot of tree cover all around the place. I'm supposed to stop on that road and meet the kidnapper, but I'll let you out before that. Take the rifle and cover me, but stay hidden. I don't believe they'll release the girl and may kill her and me. Do what you must, son."

After Jon left the car, Fr. Jake drove slowly until a van came in view. 'Aryans First' was lettered on the side.

"*So that's who it is,*" he thought. *The worst of the worse.* He estimated fifty feet, and stopped his car.

At the sound of his engine, three men came out of the van's open door. One held Dalia by the hand. She was crying. He had a revolver in his other hand. The other two held AK-47 rifles.

Fr. Jake got out of his car holding the suitcase.

The man who held Dalia walked a few paces toward the priest. "Stop there, Parson," he ordered. "You got the money?"

Fr. Jake held up the suitcase. "In here."

"Put it down." He laughed. "You were askin' who I was. Well, Parson, you tell your god, or whoever you believe in, that David Tripp had the honor of lettin' you meet him."

Tripp let go of Dalia's hand and slowly aimed his revolver at Fr. Jake as he started to mumble, "Can't leave any witnesses—"

A rifle shot echoed through the woods. Shot in the head, Tripp fell dead and let go of Dalia's hand. She ran toward Fr. Jake, who held her tightly in his arms.

Alarmed, the two men with AK- 47s brought up their weapons and looked toward the forest.

Two more rifle shots in quick succession dropped them.

Shaken, Fr. Jake made a sign of the cross toward the fallen men then put a sobbing Dalia in his car's back seat. He picked up his suitcase, put it on the car's back floor, then turned around, and drove back to meet Jon.

Jon had waited in the shelter of trees and walked over to get in the Nissan's passenger seat.

Neither mentioned the shootings, but Fr. Jake said, "Jon, we'll call the Ahmed's from the rectory to tell them their daughter is fine and to come take her home."

❧

After the phone call by Fr. Jake, during which he mentioned Jon's part in the rescue, Bahir and Amina Ahmed arrived with their son, Galeb, in a short time.

While Fr. Jake and Jon watched, Amina hugged and comforted Dalia. The priest got a blanket from his bedroom to spread around both of them. Bahir turned to shake hands with Fr. Jake and Jon, then took two envelopes from his pocket.

"Pastor," he said, "here is five hundred dollars for your church." Then he gave the other envelope to Jon. "Sir, this is five hundred dollars for you, a small enough sum for getting our daughter back, and much less than the ransom amount." Bahir waved off their thanks and said it was time to go back to their home.

❧

After the Ahmed family left, Fr. Jake brought out his bottle of French wine and two glasses from the sink cabinet.

"Jon," he said, "we could both use a glass of this. I'll call Deputy Griego about the Morada shootout. It obviously was self-defense, but I wonder if Bahir's family will have the courage to stay in Providencia?" After clinking glasses and taking a sip of wine, Fr. Jake asked, "Jon, we had talked earlier, but what do you plan to do now?"

He shrugged. "I figured I'd sell the Fort property and me and my bothers go join the Army."

"I warned you about the Afghan war back then," Fr. Jake reminded him.

"Right." Jon finished his wine and stood up. "I got me all this money now, so I guess I got a lot more thinkin' to do."

"Jon, there can't be enough thanks, even rewards, for what you did today in helping rescue that little girl."

"I appreciate that *padre*. I should be goin' back home now."

"God bless," Fr. Jake said, "and best of luck for whatever you decide."

18 aftermath of the kidnapping

Fr. Jake had barely recovered from the terror of the day's events, when he contacted Sheriff Hilario Griego about going out to the Morada. He explained what he would find there and the reason, clearly a hate crime and case of self-defense while thwarting the kidnapping of an eight-year-old girl whose parents were Muslims.

He poured himself another glass of wine and opened his Breviary to where Jon had interrupted him and finish the day's reading— Paul's letter to the Thessalonians. As usual, he read aloud.

"'Brothers, we urge and appeal to you in the Lord Jesus to make more and more progress in the kind of life you are meant to live, the life that God wants, as you learnt from us and as you are already living. You have not forgotten the instructions we gave you on the authority of the Lord Jesus.'"

He stopped reading to take a sip of wine before continuing on, when the phone rang and he picked up the receiver. "Father Jakubowski, San Isidro Church. How may I help you?"

"Pastor, this Bahir Ahmed. Again, Amina and I can't thank you enough for what you and that young man did in rescuing our daughter, but as a small token would like to invite you both to dinner at Mamacita's."

"Bahir, Jon left to go back to where he lives and try to sort out his future. You were very generous in giving him five hundred dollars."

"That was nothing, Pastor. How about joining us for that dinner? We're leaving the children with a babysitter and Dalia was asleep. You were going to introduce us to New Mexican cooking. *Comida Sabroso* you called it. I wrote it down."

"Fine. That may give us a sense of normalcy after what happened this morning."

"We also hope that might be true, and it did end in our favor. What's a good time for you, Pastor?"

"How about Five?"

"We'll be there."

☙❧

Father Jake arrived at the restaurant a few minutes after five o'clock. Bahir saw the priest and put down the menu Julia had given him, then stood to beckon him toward his table.

"*Misa' il kheer*, Pastor," he said. "That's 'good evening' in Arabic. You met Amina today."

Fr. Jake extended a hand to her. "May you both recover quickly from your terrible ordeal."

"Pastor," Bahir asked, "sit across from us, so we can talk a bit about what happened today."

"It was another hate crime," Fr. Jake told the couple. "Only by educating people about the fact that your religion, Islam, isn't a threat to this village can prevent another deadly 'incident' like today's, one I'll personally never forget."

"How can we do that?"

"We had already made a start. Cynthia Plow is planning a meeting to inform the community about Islam."

"Fine, later we can discuss how to help her." Ahmed picked up his menu. "We came here to sample New Mexico food."

To change the subject, Fr. Jake noted, "Mrs. Ahmed that's a beautiful head covering that you're wearing. Is that an Islamic custom?"

She nodded and smiled. "Yes, this one is the simplest, called *a hijab*, and leaves my face free. Two other styles have only the eyes uncovered, or conceal the face and entire body."

"It's a beautiful shade of pink."

She smiled. "My favorite color, Pastor."

Julia brought the priest a menu. "How are you, Father?"

"All right, thanks, Julia," he responded. "We want to give the Ahmed family a taste of *comida sabroso*, New Mexican cooking."

"Anything to drink? Beer or wine?"

"Nothing alcoholic…." Fr. Jake looked at the couple. "Will iced tea be all right?"

"Fine," Bahir responded.

"Coming up, Julia said. "Check out the appetizers meanwhile."

"Remember, this is on me, Pastor," Ahmed reminded him.

"Thank you." Fr. Jake turned to his wife. "Mrs. Ahmed, I —"

"Please call me Amina." she interrupted. "We lived in Albuquerque and were not so formal with friends."

"I wanted to ask if you had cooked any New Mexican dishes while you lived here."

"Not really, Pastor. We ate 'American'…beef roast, chicken, hamburger, food like that, but the wife of the Imam, my husband's, father, served traditional Islamic dishes."

"Interesting," Fr. Jake said to Bahir, "What were some of your favorites?"

"My mother made one, *Koshari*, macaroni, rice, tomato sauce…let's see, lentils, fried onions."

Julia returned with the drinks and put them in front of each one. "Any of the appetizers look good?"

Fr. Jake told her, "Give us a moment, I'm finding out about Arabic food. You may be serving some here."

Julia shrugged, without commenting. "Be back when you're ready."

The priest turned back to Bashir. "What else did you like to eat?"

"A dish made of eggs, ground beef and vegetables. For lunch, Pita bread sandwiches with lamb or chicken."

"How about dessert?"

"Not every day. I didn't mention breakfast yet. Mother served *Fatir*, a thin pastry filled with honey, but we eventually bought a toaster so toast and eggs more often than *Fatir*."

"No bacon or ham?"

"Pastor, Muslims don't eat pork." Bahir held up his menu. "Isn't this talk about food making us hungry? Let's try what New Mexicans in Providencia eat. What do you suggest, Pastor?"

"Julia thought we should have an appetizer first. Guacamole is an avocado dip eaten with chips, but tricky to handle the first time." Fr. Jake thought a moment, then recommended, "Why don't both of you try tamales and see how you like them."

"We'll do that when the waitress comes back," Bahir said, putting down his menu.

Fr. Jake paused a moment. "I hesitate to bring this up, yet people know that an Arab bought the store but nothing about you. A Pentecostal preacher named Jeremiah lives with his followers in an evangelical commune called Eden West. It's on a road not far from where you're living. Even though I'm Catholic, he tolerates me as a Christian, but I'm a little worried about his reactions to a non-Christian owning the store."

"He wouldn't dare burn—"

Fr. Jake interrupted him. "Intolerance can be deadly. As I said, to counter that, Cynthia is studying Islam and planning to make a presentation on the religion to the community. She's hoping you'll be able to attend, so I can introduce you."

Bahir Ahmed looked toward his wife. "Amina, that sounds excessive. Have we made a serious mistake in coming here? Look at what just happened to Dalia."

Fr. Jake tried to reassure them. "We don't think you did. Yours is a legitimate religion that honors God, so we should learn all we can about it. That would be a major step in fighting intolerance."

"Pastor, that does make sense." Bahir looked at his wife. "Amina, perhaps we should reconsider and go to that meeting."

"You won't be sorry," Fr. Jake told them. "The meeting starts at 7:00 p.m. but I'll get there a bit earlier. Could you come fifteen minutes sooner?"

"Yes, we'll be there by then."

19 cynthia makes her presentation on islam

On Sunday, August 29, before Mass, Cynthia Plow told Fr. Jake that she had read enough about the Islamic religion, and was now ready to plan her presentation on Islam for an evening meeting in the Elementary school. She thought that Tuesday the 31st might be enough time to inform the community and have them attend. The priest agreed; he had spoken at an August 22 Mass about the new ownership of Carlotta's by a Muslim and would today tell the congregation at Mass to mention the August meeting date to their friends and urge them to attend. It would be at 7:00 p.m.

Curious, on Monday, after eating his usual bran and banana breakfast, Fr. Jake opened his Breviary to August 31 to see if any of the readings might be relevant for the upcoming meeting.

"This First Reading is from a letter of Paul to the Thessalonians and deals with the last days. Let's see." He read aloud to himself, "'You will not be expecting us to write anything to you, brothers, about times and seasons since you know very well that the Day of the Lord is going to come like a thief in the night.'" *The end of the world is not really appropriate*, he thought. *How about the responsorial Psalm?* "'The Lord is my light and my help, whom shall I fear? The Lord is the stronghold of my life, before whom shall I shrink.' Good, that's close enough and relevant to what Muslims believe Muhammad taught about Allah…their name for God."

❧

Cynthia had asked Fr. Jake to work with her on the content of her presentation.

On Tuesday, the priest ate a quick supper, then drove over to the Elementary school to find out what she had done. When he parked his Honda Civic near the entrance, only Cynthia's Hyundai Tucson SUV and a car he guessed belonged to Mrs. Zamora, the principal, were in the parking lot.

Inside the hallway he walked past the Bi-lingual signs that reflected student conduct: RESPETO / RESPECT CHARACTER COUNTS / EL CARACTER CUENTA. A short distance further, Fr. Jake saw the principal sitting in her off ice and stopped to greet her.

"Good afternoon, Mrs. Zamora."

"Father Jakubowski." She extended a hand. "Nice to see you again. How are you?"

"Well enough," he told her, "but surprised not to see any students. Why hasn't school started?"

"Father, you must know of the recent trouble here. A Muslim Arab bought the grocery store, and an attempt was made to destroy the premises. I thought I should postpone classes until September first. Cynthia is here, in her classroom working on something."

"Yes, I came to see her. She received your permission to use her classroom this evening for a presentation to inform the community more about the Islamic religion and to fight intolerance. The Ahmed family will be there and Cynthia has material to pass out. The meeting is at Seven, but I came early to take a look at what she's done."

Mrs. Zamora nodded. "Father, I can't stay, but would like to see the material Cynthia will pass out."

"Of course. I'll leave a copy in your office."

"Thank you, Father. Have a successful evening."

When the priest entered Cynthia's classroom, she was reading an 8 x 11 printed copy of what she had written. A corner of her desk displayed two copies of the Koran in English translations, and Karen Armstrong's book, *Muhammad / A Prophet For Our Time.*

Cynthia glanced up when Fr. Jake came in. "Oh, hi, Father. I was just looking over what I wrote." She handed him the sheet. "Here, take a look."

"Sure. I see you have one of Karen Armstrong's books. Is it recent?"

"2006."

"So she's still writing. Good. In Michigan I managed to get a copy of *A History of God*, printed in 1993 and *The Battle For God*, 2001. Both have chapters about Muslims."

"Father, read the sheet I gave you," Cynthia asked. "I start out by saying that Islam is monotheistic religion, like Christianity, with a belief in one God, yet everything else I wrote is taken directly from the Koran or about what it teaches. There's information about Muhammad's life and obligations concerning the religion. Please sit down and read it back to me out loud, so I can hear how it will sound to people who come to the meeting."

"Of course, Cynthia. I'm sure you've covered everything." Fr. Jake moved a chair closer to her desk, sat down, and began to read. "Islam is a monotheistic religion, like Christianity, with belief in one God, they call Allah.

Muslims believe that the Quran, the central religious text of Islam was revealed to Muhammad by God and that he was sent to restore Islam, the monotheistic faith of Adam, Abraham, Moses and Jesus. Through the Quran the religious, social, and political tenets became the foundation of the Muslim world. The book has 114 sections covering multiple aspects of existence. Number 1, The Opening, states: "In the name of God, the Gracious, the Merciful. Praise be to God, Lord of the Worlds. The Most Gracious. The Most Merciful. Master of the Day of Judgement. It is you we Worship and upon You we call for help. Guide us to the straight path. The Path of those You have blessed, not of those against whom there is anger, nor of those who are misguided." Muhammad was born around 570 A.D. in Mecca on the Arabian Peninsula and died in 632. At the age of 40 he is said to have received his first revelation in a cave called Hira, the beginning of the tenets in the Quran, and lasted all his life. God ordered him to preach the Oness of God and to rebuke idolatry. Newly converted Muslims were persecuted and were invited to settle in Medina. Muhammad devised the beginning of the Islamic calendar there and also drew up a Constitution specifying community rights and established the first Islamic state. In 630

Muhammad and his followers retook control of Mecca. Eventually the different tribes of Arabia were unified under Islam. By Muhammad's death most of the tribes of the Arabian Peninsula had converted to Islam.

Muslims may refer to Muhammad as Prophet Muhammed or "The Prophet" or "The Messenger." They regard him as the Greatest of all Prophets, and the possessor of all virtues. Out of respect, Muslims follow the name of Muhammad with an Arabic benediction that translates as "Peace be upon Him."

Muslims have five daily prayer times, which are considered one of most important obligations of their Faith—Dawn, Midday, Afternoon, Sunset, Nighttime. Prayers remind them of Allah and an opportunity for His guidance and forgiveness. They are a bond with other Muslims worldwide. Ritual washing precedes the prayer; a rug may be used but is optional.

The Five Pillars of Faith each Muslim observes or hopes to achieve in his or her lifetime.

1. Hajj—A Pilgrimage to Mecca, Islam's holiest site.

2. Sawm—Ritual fasting during Ramadan.

3. Shahadah—There is no God but Allah and Muhammad is his Messenger.

4. Salat—Daily prayers.

5. Zakat—Donating to charity and aid to the poor."

After he finished reading, Father Jake put the sheet back on Cynthia's desk. "Splendid. You've nicely condensed Islam for your audience and I personally learned much that I didn't know. Let's be sure to invite questions for Bahir to answer." He glanced at his watch. "We probably have about twenty-five minutes before people arrive at Seven, and I told the Ahmeds to be at least fifteen minutes early. I'll go to the front entrance now and show people how to get to your classroom."

Cynthia said, "Okay, Father, but someone you know could do that and you'd be able to come back here. I have no idea about how many people might be interested enough to come, but I've added more chairs facing my desk. Four of them are for the Ahmed's. You'll want to introduce them."

꧁꧂

Around 6:40, automobiles began parking next to the school with two or three passengers getting out and heading for the entrance. Others who lived nearby walked across the lot. A few had grade school children that attended Excelencia and knew their way to the classroom. Fr. Jake dropped off a sheet that Cynthia wrote in Mrs. Zamora's office, then went to greet each person and thank them for coming. Some were his parishioners, so when he saw Armando arrive in his Camaro—without his aunt. The priest pulled him aside.

"Armando, I came here to show people how to find Cynthia's classroom, but need to make the Ahmed's feel comfortable when they arrive. Do you mind doing that?"

"Sure, Father. *No problemo.*"

"Thanks…. Oh, I see the Ahmed's getting out of their car now."

Fr. Jake went outside to escort the family in. "Welcome. I read over what Cynthia wrote about Islam and think those who come this evening will appreciate it."

"Pastor, we're a little nervous," Bahir admitted to him. "Probably not everyone will care that much about knowing our religion. Some might attend to criticize me for buying the store."

Fr. Jake replied, "I'll remind everyone it's a lesson in tolerance and its opposite is deadly. Let's go in."

Cynthia had placed a copy of her summary on each chair so everyone could read about Islam while waiting for the meeting to begin. Fr. Jake introduced the Ahmeds to Cynthia, then stood by the door, mentally counting Providenceños as they entered. *I bet we'll get 75 to attend, more than I expected,* he thought. *There's Elder Jeremiah. I didn't think the Pentecostal preacher would come. Deputy Sheriff Griego and a Deputy I don't recognize are at the back. I hope they don't expect any trouble.*

A few minutes after Seven, Fr. Jake walked to where the Ahmed family sat and announced, "Thank you, everyone, for coming this evening. I'd like to start by introducing Mister Bahir Ahmed, his wife Amina." The couple half-stood to mild, scattered applause. "Cynthia Plow, a teacher at this school, wrote the page about Islam that was on your chair. Take a moment to read it if you haven't." Applause was louder and lasted longer for a teacher many already knew. "I'm sure you have questions about Islam to ask Mister Ahmed, but let me have a minute or two first. True, this is about Islam, yet some of you have heard of the Seven Deadly Sins—Gluttony, Sloth, Anger, and so forth. Surely 'Intolerance' should be one of them. It's as deadly to the human soul as are the others. An example a week ago was an attempt to destroy the store Mister Ahmed now owns. Because of this act of intolerance, one person is dead, another arrested by Sheriff's Deputy Griego." Some in the room turned to applaud him. Fr. Jake waited, then continued, "A more recent attempt was on the life of the Ahmed's daughter, Dalia, that I witnessed. "With God's grace, that won't happen again, but only a change of heart can prevent it. Jesus taught compasssion and mercy, as did Muhammad. Let that be a lesson for all of us. Now, who has a question for Mister Ahmed?"

Elder Jeremiah raised a hand and got up. "Are you going to build a mosque here?"

Ahmed stood to answer, "Sir, I'm not an Imam, so there will not be one."

After a pause, Armando looked around, then remained seated to ask, "What is this Ra-ma-dan?"

"Sir," Ahmed explained, "Ramadan is a month of fasting from sun up to sundown and prayers during the ninth month of our lunar calendar. Muhammad reckoned months by phases of the moon, not the sun's path around the earth—"

Amina interrupted him to whisper, "Bahir, tell them about the Luna-Calendar window in Albuquerque's Old Town. They may have seen it. We did."

Bahir straightened up. "My wife refers to a chapel where a nun, Sister Giotto, crafted a glass lunar calendar widow. If you go to Albuquerque, it's worth seeing. Anything else?"

A man in back raised his hand and stood up to ask, "Do Muslim women pray on their knees like men I've seen in pictures?"

Bahir answered, "In the privacy of their home, for example, they might do so, but a Mosque has an upper galley for women."

When no one else volunteered a question, Fr. Jake looked at his watch. *After Eight, time to shut down.* "Thank you, Mister Ahmed and everyone," the priest said. "Cynthia and I hope you've had an informative evening. Drive home safely." He winked at her as the crowd began to leave and whispered. "Good job, Cynthia."

20 archbishop benisek has news for fr. jake

The next morning, before celebrating Mass, Fr. Jake walked out on his porch to check the weather, when he noticed a piece of paper on the windshield of his car, held in place by the wiper. He went down to see what it was.

Unfolding a note, he read aloud, "You want your car burned again then keep liking that Muslum." The priest looked around without expecting to see anyone. "Burned again?" he asked himself. "That's right, when my first car was torched on the Fourth of July, Armando said it wasn't an accident caused by fireworks but was deliberate. I can't remember why. Whoever wrote this must have been at the meeting last evening and misspelled Muslim. I wonder if Cynthia received any threats like this one? After Mass I'll drive over to the school and find out."

⁗

Classes would start after Labor Day, but Mrs. Zamora was in her office preparing for the opening. Fr. Jake stopped in to show her the note.

"Good morning, Father, and thanks for leaving me a copy of what Cynthia wrote. She did a marvelous job in explaining Islam. About seventy-five people came," she estimated. The priest handed her the note. "One of them left this threat on my car, and I wondered if Cynthia found anything similar."

"Threat?" After reading what the priest gave her, Mrs. Zamora stood up. "This is outrageous! Cynthia is in her classroom straightening up after last evening. Let's go ask her if she did."

Cynthia was pinning pictures on her bulletin board when the two came in.

"Father Jake. Have you recovered from last night?" she asked, half smiling.

Mrs Zamora showed her the note. "Father found this threat on his car this morning and we wondered if you received anything like it."

"Let me read it at my desk. Come on, Father." A frown formed on Cynthia's forehead as she began to read the note. Abruptly, she slapped a hand on the desk. "That's terrible! No, I've gotten nothing like that, yet it's early. I still may. Who do you believe might have written this trash?"

"I've no idea, but after the first day of school the police should be informed, and I can see to that," Mrs. Zamora offered. "Mister Ahmed probably receives similar threats every day."

"A worse one more recently," Fr. Jake said, without explaining. "Thank you. I'll let both of you know if I get more threats. It seems as if my plea for tolerance went to deaf ears."

"Only to very few, Father," Cynthia told him. "Don't be discouraged at all."

⁓⁓⁓

The threats continued, most by mail postmarked in Providencia, and then dwindled down. No damage was done to Fr. Jake's car or the store. Crazies were "letting off steam" as Cynthia put it.

Mrs. Ahmed brought her two children to the Elementary school and picked them up without incident. Still, Fr. Jake was concerned as he mulled over the threats and a few hostile remarks he had heard at the meeting.

⁓⁓⁓

A few afternoons later, Fr, Jake was mopping the floor of his kitchen, when he heard the crunch of tires on his gravel driveway. He looked out the front window and saw the white Dodge Durango of Archbishop Jan Benisek. *What could the Archbishop possibly want? He hasn't come here again since Father Mora's funeral. I met his secretary then, Father Ramón.*

He went to open the door and waited while the Archbishop, Father Ramón, and a younger priest got out of the car.

At the stairs, the Archbishop frowned. "Father Casimir, you lived in that casita when we came before, but someone else is there now. He told us you had moved to this rectory. You really should have informed me."

"I apologize, Your Excellency. Please…please come in," Fr. Jake stammered.

The Archbishop wore the same black clergy suit and Roman collar he had on his previous visit. A gold chain with a small crucifix under his suit jacket marked his ecclesiastical rank. Ramón and the other priest wore only the black suit and collar.

"Hello, Father Ramón."

"Good day, Father Casimir." He indicated the other priest. "May I introduce Father Luis Montoya."

Hispanic Fr. Jake thought, reaching to shake his hand. "A pleasure, Father."

"Same for me, Father Casimir. I learned a bit about you on the drive from Santa Fe. I understand that you're Polish, and have a parish in Michigan."

"Yes, I was ordained there in 1966, and with the unpronounceable surname of Jakubowski, for New Mexicans, anyway."

Archbishop Benisek smiled briefly at the jest, then told him, "Father Casimir, I received a phone call from Archbishop Stanley Sredzinski in Detroit. You'll recall that through our friendship he allowed you to come here to help out an ill, dysfunctional priest. Father Mora is dead now, and that was in April, about six months ago. Archbishop Stan wants you back in your parish."

"And Father Montoya will take my place here?"

"Correct.'

A chill went through Fr. Jake at the news. "Excellency, when am I to return to Michigan? I went there in early August to attend a friend's Memorial service and spoke with Archbishop Sredzinski. He wants me back, yet didn't specify a date."

"Father Casimir, you undoubtedly have affairs to clear up. This is September, so I would say within a month. That gives you time to introduce Father Montoya to your congregation."

"Father will stay here and we'll concelebrate until I leave?"

"Or each take separate Masses. Work that out between yourselves." Father Montoya has an automobile and can drive back to Providencia after we return to Santa Fe."

When Benisek stood up to leave, Fr. Jake said, "One other thing, if I may, Excellency. Cynthia Plow, a member of my congregation is of tremendous help, much like a Deacon would be. Paul cites such women helpers. I told Cynthia I'd ask your permission for her to begin training as a Deacon."

The Archbishop paused before hedging, "Oh, I'll look into it Father." He glanced at his watch. "We really must leave. While I'm here I'll check on Father Mingh down at Immaculate Conception. Introduce Father Montoya to him." Benisek signed a cross over Fr. Jake. "God bless you and keep you, Father Casimir."

"Goodbye, Excellency." He turned to the two priests. "Nice seeing you again Father Ramón, and meeting, you Father Montoya."

As he watched the three clergymen leave, Fr. Jake had not felt more depressed since he arrived at Providencia. *Do I have anything stronger than wine? I guess my suggestion for Cynthia hit a blank wall. I really need a stiff dose of whiskey.*

21 detective sonia mora returns

On Tuesday, September 8, Fr. Jake finished his usual breakfast of raisin bran and banana, then brought the cup of coffee to his armchair, sat down, and began his "Kitchen Mass" by opening his Breviary to the First Reading for that day from the Letter of Paul to the Colossians.

He read aloud, "You must live your whole life according to the Christ you have received, Jesus the Lord. You must be rooted in him and built on him and held firm by the faith you have been taught and full of thanksgiving. Make sure that no one traps you and deprives you of your freedom by some secondhand, empty, rational philosophy based on the principles of this world instead of Christ."

He had resumed reading silently when the crunch of tires in the rectory driveway and a familiar car horn he recognized sounded outside.

"Sonia is back safely from Washington. Good…" Still holding his Breviary, Fr. Jake got up to open his door for the Socorro County woman detective. Fr. Jake knew she would soon return from Washington. She had flown there for the Labor Day weekend at the invitation of Drug

Enforcement Agent Juan Hererra. He was originally an agent of the Albuquerque District DEA. Sonia met him at a meeting called to investigate drug trafficking at Fort Liberty. Afterward, she worked to help him plan the possibility of a raid on the compound. She had liked him, but Herrera had since been transferred to the DEA Washington D.C. office. Juan's invitation was a happy surprise to her.

When Sonia got out of her red 2005 Plymouth Neon, Fr. Jake met her at the door. She was not wearing her detective's uniform, but had put on a Baker-boy cap over glossy black hair.

"Welcome home, Sonia," he exclaimed, opening his arms and smiling.

"Thanks, Father." She went to give him a warm hug.

"Let's have a seat in my living room and you can tell me what happened in Washington."

"Sure thing."

When they were seated, Fr. Jake asked, "So how did everything go?"

"Super, even better than I expected," she told him.

"In what way, Sonia?"

"Juan told me he was receiving an award on September fifth for his service in the "Operation Vigilance" raid on Fort Liberty. It totally wiped out their drug smuggling operation."

"What sort of award?"

"It's called a Presidential Medal of Freedom. President Obama presented it to him in an afternoon ceremony. I wanted to be there, so booked an early Southwest Airlines 'Red Eye' flight to Ronald Reagan Airport in Washington. It's about a three-hour flight. Then I took a taxi to the DEA building on K Street. Juan met me there, and we had a quick lunch before the ceremony. He told me a few statistics about the Agency. They have over 5000 special agents spread out nationwide, a similar support staff, and three billion dollar budget this year. The building is of about seven stories—"

"Sonia, would you like coffee?" Fr. Jake interrupted.

"Sure, Father, I'm babbling on."

"No, no, I'm very interested. I'll bring it in."

When he returned from the kitchen with the beverage, the priest asked Sonia why, aside from the ceremony, Juan had summoned her.

"Father, the Agency doesn't have many female agents. He…he wants me to be one of them."

"If you accept, you'll leave New Mexico."

"True, yet it would be an opportunity for advancement I'd never have again."

"*Vaya con Dios*, Sonia."

She nodded thanks, and continued, "Juan figured I'd accept and introduced me to a mentor, Frank Belisarius, to show me the ropes. Juan lives in an apartment a block from the Agency and thinks there would be one available for me. We didn't discuss salary, but it would be more than I'm making now."

"When would you start?"

"In about a month, on October first. That gives me time to settle affairs in Socorro."

Fr. Jake reached for her hand. "Need I say that you'll be sorely missed?"

"I know, my entire life has been here." Sonia paused to sip her coffee, then said, "Father, after the medal ceremony I spoke a bit with President Obama. He's…'cool'…I guess that's the current word. He asked me about my background, my detective work here, and wished me well with the Agency." Sonia put down her cup and stood up to stretch her arms. "I should go now. Needless to say I have a lot to do before October. Oh, one more rather important thing." She took an engagement ring from her purse and held it up. "Juan proposed marriage and I want us to come back here and have you marry both of us."

"*Superbo*, but Sonia, I was just told I had to return to Michigan around that time. Another priest, Father Montoya, will take over San Isidro."

"Don't worry, Father," she countered, and took a pocket calendar from her purse. "Set a day during the last week in September and we'll fly in for our wedding."

He studied her calendar. "How about midweek, September 23? It's a Thursday. Ten o'clock, but come to the rectory at least an hour earlier."

"That would be great, Father."

"Okay, Sonia. I've not performed a wedding since I came here, but look forward to officiating at your marriage ceremony."

"Thanks, Father. I really should leave now, and I'll tell Juan about the September date."

"Fine." Fr. Jake placed his hands on Sonia's head. May Almighty God bless you in the name of the Father, and of the Son and the Holy Spirit."

Both responded, "Amen."

With sadness he watched Sonia leave. They had worked well together in solving several crimes and would not see each other again after her wedding. He would be in Michigan by then.

22 sonia mora and juan hererra marry

Sonia and Juan's Southwest Airlines flight left Washington at 2:00 p.m. on Wednesday and arrived at the Albuquerque Sunport by late afternoon. Both had only carry-on luggage. He rented a car and knew the drive to Providencia on I-25 would take about an hour. They decided to rent a room at the Bellemonte Motel in Belén, and eat supper there rather than bother Father Jake at night.

⇦⇨

On Thursday morning, the couple arrived at Fr. Jake's rectory a few minutes before nine o'clock.

The priest greeted them warmly at the door, shaking their hands.

"Sonia, Juan, how good to see you both again. Can I get you coffee before we talk?"

"Thanks, Father,' Sonia replied. "We had breakfast at the motel."

"Then let's sit in the living room."

"Fine with us," Sonia told him.

After they were seated, Fr. Jake said, "First off, I'm flattered…well, happy may be a better word, happy that you wanted me to officiate at your wedding."

"Father," Juan told him, "Sonia and I wouldn't want it any other way."

"My appreciation to you both. I've read about a Wedding Mass in my Breviary, and have a few questions I must ask, and then I'll walk you through the ceremony at the church."

"As the saying goes, we're ready and probably able Father," Sonia told him. "Go ahead."

"Are both of you Catholic?"

"We are."

"Have either of you been married before and afterward divorced?"

"No."

Fr. Jake smiled. "Looks like you passed with ease, so let's walk over to the church."

"Lead on, Father."

Inside San Isidro the priest said, "Let's sit in this pew while I explain. Actually, here are two Catholic marriage ceremonies. One is a Nuptial Mass, which is quite long and fancy, with a lot of readings from the Old and New Testaments. Singing hymns. Bridesmaids. Best Man, and so on."

"What's the other?" Sonia quickly wanted to know.

"It's called A Celebration of Marriage and is more like a regular Sunday Mass. Sonia, did you happen to bring a wedding dress?"

"Father, I bought a very simple white one."

"I have a tuxedo," Juan added.

"Good, then let's opt for that service." Fr. Jake stood up. "Sonia, you'll start at the church entrance and process down the aisle to the altar. Juan will be waiting there. Cynthia will have a bouquet of flowers for you to hold and—"

"Don't overdo, Father," she interrupted.

"You'll exchange wedding rings?"

"Of course," Sonia responded, "I've attended weddings and know the routine."

"Fine, let's go to the rectory where you both can change clothes. I'll return to vest at the church. Come back when you're ready. Juan, a separate *segrario* is attached to the church. You can see it from here. Enter that way and stand with me by the altar."

"I'll do that, Father."

Fr. Jake looked with renewed interest at Juan as he walked hand-in-hand with Sonia, his bride-to-be. *He's a least a half foot taller than Sonia, dark brown hair cut short. Rather heavy eyebrows on a strong angular face. Very handsome. Love shows in his eyes as he smiles at Sonia.*

❧

No formal wedding invitations had been sent out, but some residents of the village had walked to the church for the service. Now the San Isidro parking lot rapidly filled up with the cars of others who knew the woman detective and wanted to attend her wedding. Deputy Hilario Griego and another Sheriff's officer directed traffic.

Fr. Jake put on a white chasuble and looked at the pews. Armando sat near the front with his aunt Ofila. Cynthia had driven back to the Equus sanctuary and brought Dulci to attend the wedding. He was surprised to see Mrs. Ahmed and her two children sitting in the last pew.

Cynthia had been talking to Dulci when she saw Fr. Jake enter and went to over to him.

"Father, I have a camera and can take photos of the wedding."

"Good, I'm sure they will appreciate them."

"This is a surprise, Father, but Mister Ahmed has offered to pay for a luncheon at Mamacita's after the wedding. He bought a cake, too."

"Very generous of him, Cynthia," Fr. Jake said, "but a lot of people are coming to attend the wedding."

"Not everyone's invited, only those who know Sonia well. I made tickets to pass out—" Applause as the congregation stood made both look toward the Church entrance. "Oh, here she is. I'll go give her that bouquet."

Sonia wore the white wedding dress she mentioned, but without a train at the hem. She took Cynthia's flowers, smiled thanks, and walked slowly toward the altar. Fr. Jake and Juan watched her come and stand in front of them.

As at all Masses, Fr. Jake began with the sign of the cross. "In the name of the Father, and of the Son, and of the Holy Spirit. Amen. Let us pray."

"A reading from Psalm 19:3.5. 'May the Lord send you help from his holy place and from Zion may he watch over you. May he grant you your heart's desire and lend his aid to all your plans.'

In Ephesians, Paul writes, 'Christ loves his church and he sacrificed himself for her so that she could become like a holy and untouchable bride.' Amen."

"Dear friends, we are gathered here to witness the marriage of Juan Hererra and Sonia Mora. Let us pray." Fr. Jake read from a book he held. "'Father, you have made the bond of Marriage a holy mystery, a symbol of Christ's love for his Church. Hear our prayers for Juan and Sonia. With faith in you and in each other they pledge their love today. May their lives always bear witness to the reality of that love.'" He looked up at Juan. "Do you take Sonia to be your wife and promise to be true to her in sickness and in health, and love and honor her all the days of your life?"

"I do," he replied.

"Sonia, do you take Juan to be your husband and promise to be true to him in sickness and in health all the days of your life?"

"I do," she also replied.

Fr. Jake had their rings and asked them to place them on each other's fingers, then made a sign of the cross over their heads. "I now pronounce you man and wife. Go in peace to love and serve the Lord."

The congregation applauded as Juan took Sonia in his arms for the wedding kiss.

Cynthia took her photos and then stood aside as an altar girl to assist Fr. Jake, until the Final Blessing at the conclusion of Mass.

After Juan and Sonia knelt on mats at one side of the altar, the priest addressed the congregation.

"We will celebrate with a Mass that includes Holy Communion. If you are a baptized Catholic you may partake of the bread and wine. If not, come up with your arms crossed and I'll give you a blessing." With slight smile he added, "Of course, that's not obligatory."

The Mass continued with the day's readings, Consecration of the bread and wine into the body and Blood of Christ, and final Gospel.

Everyone stood when Fr. Jake faced the congregation at the altar and prayed, "The Mass is ended. In the name of the Father, and of the Son, and of the Holy Spirit, go and serve the Lord. Amen."

After the couple passed, Armando asked his aunt Ofilia, "Wasn't the *detectiva* beautiful, auntie?"

"*Detectiva?*"

"Sonia, the bride."

"Mando, *porque* you no marry?"

"Aw, I'm in love with cars, auntie. You know that."

"You should marry," she grumbled.

Dulci, sitting in the pew behind, heard them. "My father probably would have felt the same way."

"You don't have a boyfriend?" Armando asked her.

"No, but I sort of like the guy who delivers hay for my horses. He owns a stallion, so we have something in common. He stays awhile sometimes, and we talk."

"*Buena suerte*, good luck," he told Dulci. "Now let's go eat."

Fr. Jake had followed the newlyweds to the entrance of the church. Cynthia joined him shortly after, to give tickets to those in the congregation—Dulci, Armando, his aunt Ofilia, and a few teachers from her school. Both waited until Sonia and Juan had again been congratulated, mostly by friends, then took them aside.

"Mister Ahmed has lunch ready at Mamacita's with even a wedding cake. Not everyone here could possibly be invited so I've passed out a few tickets. You can go on ahead with me."

"That's kind of Ahmed," Sonia said, then quipped, "Father Jake, it seems that your presentation on Islam is bearing both fruit *and* cake."

"Praised be to God!" he jovially exclaimed.

Cynthia joined them. "I'm finished giving out tickets, Father. There weren't that many people I know, but I'm sure a few others heard about a free lunch and might barge in."

"We'll let them stay," Fr. Jake said.

"Juan parked our car rental here," Sonia said. "Father, Cynthia, you can drive to the restaurant with us."

❧

At the restaurant, Fr. Jake introduced Juan and Sonia to Ahmed and his wife, Amina.

"We congratulate you also," Ahmed told them, then turned to the priest. "Pastor, I have set up a head table for you and the groom and bride, with the cake and two bottles of Champagne, even though we will not drink. We have a pitcher of sweetened iced tea. There is soda for children."

"Bahir," Fr. Jake said, "I saw the Arabic food at the buffet. Can you tell us what it is if everyone comes over?"

"Ah, yes. Much is finger food in Phyllo bread, easy to eat."

"Sonia, Juan," he called out. "Come and choose your lunch."

At the table, Ahmed pointed to one dish. "Here you have Shakishka, eggs, ground beef and vegetables. Next is Goulash, the bread stuffed with beef, cheese, and spinach. The most difficult to make is Koshari…macaroni, rice, lentils, fried onions, all in a tomato sauce."

Fr. Jake asked, 'What are these round puff balls?"

"You are at the dessert, Pastor. Puffs are filled with honey or melted chocolate. Perhaps all here will not like this food so over there on the table are American grilled cheese sandwiches—"

A pop-pop sound at the head table alerted them; Amina had opened the champagne.

Ahmed reacted, "Shouldn't we now go back and toast our newlyweds?"

Four champagne flutes surrounding the wedding cake sparkled with the beverage. Two glasses had iced tea, Ahmed indicated where everyone should stand, then handed each their drink. Fr. Jake noted there was no Bridgroom-Bride figure on the cake. *Because Muhammad destroyed idols?* he wondered.

"A Muslim wedding is not like yours," Ahmed told everyone, "but as the ritual said, we wish you, Juan and Sonia, health and happiness." Glasses clinked all around, then everyone sipped their drinks.

I have no speech to make," Ahmed announced, holding up a sheet of paper, "yet am familiar with words of one of your Christian holy men, Francis of Assis. I shall read them now. 'Lord…Allah the Merciful…make me an instrument of your peace. Where there is hatred, let me sow love. Where there is injury, pardon. Where there is doubt, faith. Where there is despair, hope. Where there is darkness, light. Where there is sadness, joy. Grant that I may not so much seek to be consoled as to console, to be understood as to understand, to be loved as to love. For it is in giving that we receive, in pardoning that we are pardoned and it is in dying that we are born to eternal life.'"

Ahmed put the paper down. "What Muslim who has endured intolerance could not value these words?" After a pause, while those attending clapped agreement, he said, "Now, let the bride cut the cake, then all shall eat. Oh, one other word, please." He indicated the two Muslim families sitting at their tables. "Doctor Alawi Alvi is a surgeon." The man half-rose to bow. "Doctor Ata Assan is a dentist." He nodded and waved a hand. "Both practice in Belèn. If you have any such needs, take one of their cards, or talk to them. Now go and fill your plates!"

The meal proceeded jovially with everyone tasting and enjoying the Arabic food.

After dessert, Sonia took Fr. Jake aside. "Juan and I agree that was a most wonderful marriage ceremony you planned for us. Thank you again."

"Least I could do, Sonia. I've said that I'll never see you again."

"Come on, Father, I certainly will return to Providencia for some reason."

"Guess I haven't told you yet that Archbishop Benisek came to see me a few days ago. His Excellency introduced me to Father Luis Montoya, a younger priest he brought with him from Santa Fe."

"*Hispano.*"

"Yes. The Archbishop reminded me that I was asked to come out here to help your uncle, Father Mora, at San Isidro. I'm no longer needed for that, and my own Archbishop wants me back in Michigan to run my parish there. Father Montoya will be my replacement."

After a stunned silence at the unexpected news, Sonia ventured, "When is this Father Montoya supposed to be here?"

"Before Sunday I hope. I'll introduce him to my congregation at that day's 8:00 a.m. Mass."

"I'll be in Washington by then and won't meet that priest."

"Too bad, Sonia, but I think Father Montoya will do well here," Fr. Jake told her.

23 fr. jake's last mass

Father Luis Montoya drove into the gravel parking space of the rectory and parked behind Fr. Jake's Nissan in the late afternoon of that Saturday, September 25. Fr. Jake was preparing a kind of farewell homily for Sunday, when he heard a car arrive and guessed it was Montoya. He met him at the door. The priest wore a colorful summer shirt.

"Welcome, Father. I hope you had an easy drive," he said. "Bring in your suitcase."

After handshakes were exchanged, Montoya said, "I made good time getting here, no traffic jams on I-25."

"Good. Have you eaten supper?"

"Thanks, I stopped at a MacDonald's in Las Lunas."

Fr. Jake told him, "A glass of wine wouldn't hurt, while I show you around your new rectory. We can sit and talk a bit first. Of course, I'll introduce you at the two masses tomorrow, but you also can say something to the congregation if you want."

"Thank you. It won't be much of a homily."

"No, not a sermon, I meant a little about you as a newly ordained priest. Didn't you celebrate Mass in Albuquerque?"

"I was assistant pastor a short while at Saint Bernard's before the Archbishop decided to send me to replace you in Providencia."

"I see. Let me bring our wine." *I like him, youngish face, slim, not pretentious. Will they like him here?* Fr. Jake came back from the refrigerator with a three-quarter-full bottle of Côtes du Rhone and two glasses. "This isn't sacramental wine," he said, "and I'm not much of a cook. I mostly heat up frozen foods and don't normally drink wine with dinner." He poured wine in the two glasses, handed the priest one, and clinked it. "Cheers, *Na Zdtowie.*"

"That's Polish," Montoya said after taking a sip. "The Archbishop told me you were born there."

"True, and how I got to Michigan is a long story for another time. I need to know more about you and for you to talk about at Mass tomorrow."

"Father, I went to Saint Bartholomew school in Albuquerque. When I became an altar boy, the priest there took an interest in me and suggested I attend a Seminary after graduation. I always was interested in religion and followed his advice."

"And here you are. Do you speak Spanish?" Fr. Jake asked. "*Habla Español?*"

"Well, not fluently. My grandparents came to America from Mexico and probably did speak Spanish, but my own parents only spoke English at home."

"No matter, not many here speak Spanish. As Armando, an auto mechanic you'll meet at Mass tomorrow puts it, 'Only the *viejos*…the oldsters…when they don't want you to know who they're gossiping about.'"

After laughing, Montoya, said, "Tell me, Father, is this a sleepy little town without much excitement? Is that why Archbishop Benesik sent me here as my first Parish?"

The priest took another sip of wine to suppress a smile. "Current 'excitement' is that a Muslim bought the only grocery store with a gas station for miles around. Bahir Ahmed was born in Albuquerque, His father is Imam at an Islamic mosque there."

"I'm not that familiar with the religion."

"The sale has stretched the toleration limit for a Muslim and his family to a few of the villagers living in Providencia. Ahmed is a compassionate, hard-working man. I hope you can meet him before I leave." Fr. Jake finished his wine and stood up. "Now let me show you your compact little rectory." He led the way from the kitchen to the living room. "Unfortunately, there is only one bedroom, so you'll have to draw straws to see which guest will sleep on the couch. That will be you tonight. Bathroom is on the left, where I put your suit case. Our first Mass is at 8:00 a.m."

❧❧

Fr. Jake was up at Six, fed cut-up bread to his birds, and set out two bowls of raisin bran with a couple of over-ripe bananas and a pitcher of milk alongside. A coffee cup was ready to be filled. He had begun to read his Breviary at the kitchen table when, shortly after, he heard Father Montoya's portable alarm go off. *I'll wait until he's dressed and comes in here to have breakfast.*

Montoya wore his black clergy suit and collar, had shaved, and looked well-groomed when he entered the kitchen. "Good morning, Father Jaku… Jakubowski is what the Archbishop told me that was your Polish name."

Fr. Jake put down the Breviary and looked up. "Good morning, Father Montoya. That was a perfect pronunciation and I trust you slept well."

"Quite well, thank you."

"I'm offering you my standard breakfast…." He indicated the cereal bowls. "Help yourself, but you may prefer bacon and eggs, so after Mass I'll take you to the store and introduce you. You'll be buying your food there."

"This is fine." Montoya sat down and silently crossed himself before cutting up the banana into his cereal.

Crossing myself before eating is something I never do in the morning, Fr. Jake thought.

"I have only three chasubles in a vesting alcove at San Isidro White, Purple and Green that I wear," he said between eating his cereal. "They may not be correct for the Ordinary of the Season, but you can wear one. When I asked the Archbishop if we would be concelebrating Mass, he said we should decide that."

"I've never concelebrated one, Father."

"It's not difficult," Fr. Jake told him. "I'll do the Elevation and you basically stand next to me.

Cynthia Plow, an elementary school teacher, helps me as an altar girl… woman…I should say. You'll meet her."

Montoya pushed his bowl aside. "I meant to ask you about a small shrine with a wooden statue I saw in your living room. It has flowers and a candle on it."

"My *Altarcito*," Fr. Jake explained. "The statue is San Isidro, patron saint of our church. Ofilia, a parishioner's aunt, told me to call on the saint if I had a problem, which I did at the time. Light the candle, arrange the flowers, and pray for a solution, she told me."

"Isn't that a form of superstition?"

Fr. Jake replied, "Father Montoya, call it what you will yet aren't Catholics told to pray for the answer to a problem?" He looked at his watch. "Let's go over to the church now."

In San Isidro, Cynthia had brought the wine and water cruets to a table on the left side of the altar and was about to bring a water bowl and towel, when the two priests entered.

"Good morning, Father Jake," she greeted and nodded toward the other priest.

"Cynthia, this is Father Luis Montoya."

Montoya extended a hand. "I'm so pleased to meet you, Cynthia. Father told me what a help you are to him."

After shaking hands, she asked, "Father Montoya, are you a visiting priest or a friend of our pastor?"

"Neither, Cynthia," Fr. Jake answered for him. "Father Montoya will be your new priest here at San Isidro."

"What? I…I don't understand—"

"He'll concelebrate with me today. I'll introduce him to the congregation and explain more after the Gospel." Fr. Jake looked toward the entrance. "We should vest now, Father Montoya. People are starting to come in."

As usual, Armando and his aunt Ofilia sat in the first pew, Cynthia sat in the pew behind, too stunned to tell them what she had just heard about having a new priest.

Instead of processing to the altar from the entrance, Fr. Jake came out from the vestry with Father Montoya and stood with him, facing the congregation at the foot of the altar stair.

"May I introduce Father Luis Montoya, who will be your new Pastor and will concelebrate Mass with me today. After the Gospel, Father will tell you something about himself. Please stand."

At rustle of clothing, both priests turned to face the altar and kneel while reciting the opening prayer of the Mass.

"In the name of the Father, and of the Son, and of the Holy Spirit. Amen."

❧

After the Gospel reading, Father Montoya climbed the pulpit stairs and paused before announcing, "Catholics of San Isidro Church, I consider it my privilege to have been chosen to serve as your Pastor. I was informed that Father Jaku…Jakubowski was only assigned here on a temporary basis, and that he must return to Michigan. We have a church bulletin and I will have my biography printed in that. You will soon enough get to know me." Amid chuckles, he gestured towards Fr. Jake, sitting in the chair he used while Cynthia read the daily readings. "Father…," he said, then came down the pulpit stairs.

Fr. Jake whispered thanks to him in passing, mounted the stairs, and looked over the congregation. "Today my remarks will not be a homily on the Gospel or liturgical season, just personal recollections. At a Mass in June, I called you *Mi buenos amigos*, and, indeed, many of you have become my good friends. As your Pastor, I can look back on my time here as one of the most rewarding times in my long life. I was sent here to help your former priest, Father Jesus Mora, God rest his soul. As an outsider, neither Hispanic nor New Mexican, I was gently warned that you would not like me. Further, my surname, Jakubowski, is a mouthful, so my friend Armando there gave it a Spanish twist as 'Father Hakub'."

Armando grinned, looked around, and pumped a fist.

Fr. Jake smiled at him, then continued. "Cynthia Plow energized San Isidro and became a fine Acolyte. Today everyone living in Providencia faces the challenge of not discriminating against the family of the Muslim gentleman who bought Carlotta's store. There already have been several, one that could have ended in the death of their daughter. Cynthia recently made a fine presentation about the Islamic faith that many of you attended. Intolerance is a deadly sin that can spawn violence. It did so when a man tried to destroy the gasoline pumps at the store and was killed. Even I received death threats." Fr. Jake paused before continuing. "I thank all of you for becoming *Mi amigos*. My request now is that you accept Father Montoya and support him in the many challenges that face him. Now let us continue the Mass. Amen."

❧

After Mass ended, Armando followed Fr. Jake out and pulled him aside.

"Father Hakub," he offered, "I'll buy your Nissan and drive you to Albuquerque to catch your flight back to Michigan."

"Thanks, that's very kind of you Armando. So, what did you think of Father Montoya?"

He glanced around, then leaned closer to whisper, "Father, they ain't gonna like him."

"Armando," Fr. Jake gently reprimanded, "that's what you said when I came here, and you were wrong. Let's hope to God you're wrong again."

About the Author

An artist and writer, Albert Noyer was born in Switzerland but raised in Detroit, Michigan. After Army service, he pursued degrees in art, art education, and teaching humanities, at Wayne State University. He subsequently worked as a commercial artist, taught art in a Detroit Public Schools technical/vocational program, and art history at a private college. Noyer retired to New Mexico with his wife, Jennifer, where he exhibits watercolor paintings and woodcut prints in galleries and regional exhibits. His artwork has been featured in *New Mexico Magazine* and the *Mature Life in New Mexico* supplement in Sunday's *Albuquerque Journal*. He is a member of the New Mexico Watercolor Society, SouthWest Writers, Sisters in Crime, Croak & Dagger, and New Mexico Veteran's Art.

Published by Plain View Press, his contemporary Fr. Jake Mysteries, *The Ghosts of Glorieta*; *One for the Money, Two for the Sluice*; and *Deadly Discrimination* are set in Michigan and New Mexico. The two volume *Alberix the Celt*, also published by Plain View Press, is a retelling of Julius Caesar's conquest of Gaul from the viewpoint of a Celtic youth caught up in the Romanization of the country now called France. Noyer first published A.D. fifth century novels, the *Getorius* and *Arcadia* mysteries, set in an era seen as critical in creating the political, religious, and cultural institutions that survive into modern times.

www.ingramcontent.com/pod-product-compliance
Lightning Source LLC
Chambersburg PA
CBHW060556100726
47907CB00005B/1383